Never Again

Brody Connor
Book 1

Monty R. Garner

WOLFPACK
PUBLISHING
— EST 2013 —

Never Again
Paperback Edition
Copyright © 2025 by Monty R. Garner

Wolfpack Publishing
1707 E. Diana Street
Tampa, FL 33610

www.wolfpackpublishing.com

Paperback ISBN 979-8-89567-798-8
Ebook ISBN 979-8-89567-797-1
LCCN 2025948119

Never Again

Chapter One

DR. JONATHAN MELROSE FINISHED APPLYING the dressing to Miss Willow Hunter's arm, which she had cut with a butcher knife while cutting up a chicken. The doctor sewed the cut together using seven stitches while the older lady sobbed from the pain.

Dr. Melrose talked as he worked. "Willow, don't get the bandage wet, and leave it on for a few days. Come back in a week to ten days, and I'll remove the stitches."

"Thank you, Doctor. May I have a little something for the pain?"

Dr. Melrose turned his head to the open door to his operating room, where all his medication was kept. "Thaddeus, bring a container of laudanum and an empty bottle. Willow needs some to take home with her."

The young man, wearing an apron over the front of his clothing, came into the room and followed the doctor's instructions. "How much do you want me to transfer into the bottle, Doctor?"

"Two tablespoons should be sufficient." Dr. Melrose looked at the woman. "Only take a half teaspoon when you get home and another at bedtime." The doctor's assistant handed the lady the medication and took hold of her arm to help her off the bed.

Willow slid off the examination bed, held her arm, which was in pain, and left the room. "Thank you, Doctor. Thaddeus, tell your mama I said hi."

"Yes, ma'am," said the boy, and returned to the room he had come from earlier.

"Thaddeus, hold up," said the doctor. "I'm finished for the day. Take this needle with you and put it with the other instruments you're going to sterilize. Go ahead and take these bloody towels and put them in the basket. They can wait until tomorrow."

"Yes, sir, Doctor," said the boy, picking up the needle along with the towels and going back into the room.

Thaddeus was a kind, compassionate young man who had worked for the doctor for the past two years after school and on weekends. Standing six feet tall and weighing one hundred seventy pounds, the young man kept his long blonde hair combed and used a rag tied as a headband. He dressed appropriately to the doctor's standards, which were clean clothes, long-sleeve shirts, and nice britches.

Thaddeus finished his work for the day and will be back shortly after daylight tomorrow since it is Saturday. Two days earlier, the young man graduated from the twelfth grade with the best grades in his class.

Thaddeus aspires to attend Kansas City Medical College, a new school that only a few students have the honor of attending. He saved his money, and Dr. Melrose helped him by writing letters to the college for admission.

The doctor's assistant removed his apron and threw it in with the soiled towels. He would wash them in the morning and hopefully get to do medical work on a few of the patients. Sometimes the doctor lets him stitch up a cut or apply splints and plaster to a broken arm or leg. He had assisted in more than half a dozen childbirths and even a few gunshot wounds. Most ailments that came in were colds, stomachaches, cuts, and broken bones.

Twice, he had assisted the doctor in the operating room. Once to remove a gallbladder and once when a woman was having difficulty with natural childbirth, and the doctor had to operate and take the baby from the woman's stomach.

Thaddeus couldn't wait to move off and get away from the home life he had. His stepfather, Ludwig Muller, was a mean, abusive man who had beaten him and his mother multiple times over the past five years.

The young man walked on eggshells when he was around the man who was four inches taller and outweighed him by seventy pounds. Ludwig earned his living owning and operating a tavern at Second and Waco Streets in Wichita, Kansas. He was not a man to mess with, and the men he associated with were just as bad.

Thaddeus could hear his mother's screams as he came down the walkway to the front door of their residence. Rushing to the door and throwing it open to see Ludwig hitting his mother, whose face was already bruised and bloody.

"I'm going to kill you," screamed Thaddeus, and jumped onto the back of his stepfather. His left arm went around the man's neck so he wouldn't fall off, and he commenced to hit the abusive man on the side of his face.

"Get off me, you little hoodlum," shouted Ludwig, reaching up with his right arm to block the punches, grabbed Thaddeus by his hair, bent over, and threw the boy to the floor. A huge right fist lashed out and connected to the side of the boy's head.

Ludwig took hold of Thaddeus's shirt and jerked him up to punch him in the solar plexus that knocked the air from the boy's lungs. Then, a bombardment of rights and lefts hit the boy until he was unconscious on the floor.

Thaddeus opened his eyes some minutes later to see his mother over him with a wet rag, wiping the blood from his face. "Baby, I'm so sorry. Are you seriously hurt anywhere?"

He sat up and said, "I'm going to live. How are you?"

She smiled through broken and bruised lips. "I'll live. You know how Ludwig gets when you try to protect me. I'm afraid that one of these days, he'll kill you. I want you to move out as soon as you can."

Thaddeus began getting up off the floor. "I will, but I want you to come with me." He grimaced as he stood and raised his shirt to see a bruise the size of a cantaloupe on his stomach.

Ellen, his mother, wiped a spot of blood off his lip. "You know I can't leave. He would come after me and kill you."

Thaddeus pointed to the backyard. "I'm going out back to sit until supper. Will Ludwig return for supper tonight?"

Ellen lowered her head. "No, I told him we were having soup, and that's why he hit me. He wanted beef and beans."

Thaddeus put his arm around his mama's neck. "Mama, I'll figure something out to get you out of here." The bruised boy went out the back door.

Thaddeus sat in one of the chairs scattered around a

giant oak tree where he spent his evenings to escape the Kansas heat. He sat thinking about his future and began to form a plan. Tomorrow, after work, he would start putting things in place to make his escape from the violence that he had endured for the past five years.

Thaddeus's father, Connor Malloy, had died in a fight at the cattle shipping pens when he got into a scuffle with a cowboy who had brought a herd up the Chisholm Trail. The devastation to his family was something that would scar Thaddeus for the rest of his life. Three months later, Ellen married Ludwig, who was nice to the boy and his ma for the first six months. The hostility started as mostly verbal aggression and advanced to physical abuse.

The boy hated the man and everything he stood for, and today was the last time he would ever be beaten.

Now, all he had to do was research where he could go and what he would need to get there. Hopefully, he can talk to Dr. Melrose tomorrow and put his plan together soon.

When it was dark, the boy entered the house and ate his supper silently. He had a lot on his mind and couldn't share it with his mother yet.

After supper, Thaddeus bathed and laid out clothes for tomorrow's work. The young man knew to be quiet when leaving the house in the early morning, or he would get another beating if he woke up the evil man. Ludwig closed his tavern late at night and slept during the day.

Chapter Two

THADDEUS HAD ALREADY WASHED THE USED towels and sheets when Dr. Melrose came in the following morning, sipping coffee out of a mug when the assistant turned to greet the physician. "Good morning, Doctor."

"Hello Thaddeus. By that black eye, I have to assume that Ludwig beat up your mother and you again."

Thaddeus dried his hands on his apron. "Yes, sir. I tried to defend her, but he got the best of me. Doctor, can I talk to you about something?"

"Of course, follow me to my office."

Thaddeus took a seat. "If someone left here and never wanted to be found, where would they go?"

"I'm not sure what you need this information for, but if you want to get your mother away where Ludwig would never find her, I suggest you go south into Indian Territory, where there is unassigned land," said the doctor. "The reason is, the president is considering a land run where people can claim land of their own."

"Do you know where this unassigned land is or when the land run will be?" asked Thaddeus.

"I know it's due south of Kansas in the middle of the Territory, stretching south to the North Canadian River. If a man's already there, he can come away with some mighty good property, and no one would know who you are if you change your and your mother's names."

Thaddeus leaned forward. "What would be the most common way to get there?"

Dr. Melrose put a finger to his chin. "Well, I would say by horseback or by a wagon. But someone could follow you and catch up to you fast. You could also take the train, but again, your whereabouts could be tracked. A person might be able to take a boat down the Arkansas River for a ways and then get a couple of horses to ride the rest of the way."

"If someone did decide to head out to Indian Territory, what things would he need to take?"

The doctor leaned back in his chair. "He would need a skillet, canteen, food, a large knife, and a gun to kill game to eat. He would also need a bedroll and maybe a needle and thread. I would take some medical supplies in case of a cut or snake bite."

"Thanks, Doctor, for talking to me. I'm not sure what to do, but whatever it is, I need to plan it out."

"Thaddeus, you plan it wisely. I still think you'll make a great doctor someday."

Thaddeus returned to work and occupied his mind with his plan to leave home.

———

IMMEDIATELY AFTER WORK, he walked west to the river and checked out the banks, looking for a boat or canoe that he could take. He wanted one with a paddle and one that didn't leak water.

He spied a lovely wooden boat partially pulled upon the soft sandbank two hundred feet downstream from where he stood. He walked to the boat and pushed it into the water to see if it leaked. The boat had two paddles, three fishing poles, fishing line, and hooks that someone used to fish. The young man pulled the boat back in place and walked to the business section of Wichita.

Thaddeus purchased a small skillet, a small pan, a large knife in a holster, a canteen, and a ground tarp. He could take some other items he would need, like a spoon, fork, and quilts, from home.

Ludwig had gone to the tavern by the time the young man arrived home. Thaddeus ate his supper, and his mother came in, dressed differently tonight. He looked at her and asked, "Where're you going?"

"I have to help your father at the tavern. He's short-handed and demanded that I come help."

Thaddeus dropped his spoon on the table. "That sorry excuse of a man is not my father. I hate his guts."

Ellen put her hand on his cheek. "I know, and you'll be going off to doctor college soon. Just try not to be around him if you can." She walked out the door.

Thaddeus went into the room where Ludwig slept and started searching the room for money and guns. He found one hundred and twenty dollars under the mattress and a gun in one of the drawers in the dresser. The weapon was a Colt, .41 caliber Thunderer, and it came with two boxes of shells and a holster.

Thaddeus took the gun, shells, and money to the kitchen and put them in a used flour sack. He needed to find a place to hide his things, and he thought about the shed out back. It was made so he could get to it without going through the house.

The young man spent his Sunday washing his clothes like he did every Sunday and stayed away from his stepfather. He found a leather bag in the shed and used it to put his clothes in, which he would take with him.

———

MONDAY CAME AROUND, and the young man had everything he needed for his trip except food. He thought about what to take and decided on cornmeal, flour, bacon, salt, and a few cans of beans. He wanted to go as light as possible and aimed to catch fish on the river as he made his way south.

Work was great on Monday, and he kept occupied helping the doctor treat various injuries of the townsfolk. When Thaddeus was finally finished at work, the doctor said, "I'm assuming that you will take off without a lot of notice, so I'm going to pay you daily in case you decide to leave town without warning."

Thaddeus took the money. "Thanks, Dr. Melrose."

On his way home, he calculated his money, adding what he had stolen from Ludwig to one hundred sixty-one dollars. That might be enough to buy himself a horse later.

The house was quiet when he walked up the path to the door and opened it. "Mama, I'm home," called out Thaddeus. There was no answer, and he assumed that she was working at the tavern again. There was a pot on the stove, and it was still cooking. If she was working, why did she leave the pot on the stove?

Thaddeus took off as fast as he could and rushed into the bedroom, where his mother lay on the floor, bloodied and unconscious. He ran to the kitchen, wet a towel, and returned to start cleaning the blood off her face and get his mama awake. She brought her hand up to the rag as he washed off blood. "Mama, can you hear me?"

She nodded her head and tried to lift it. "Lay still until I can examine you to see if anything is broken. He felt along her arms and legs, but she didn't cry out, so he lifted the shirt she had on, and her stomach and right rib cage were severely bruised.

"You may have some cracked ribs. Let me help you up so you can lay on the bed." He sat his mother up, put his hands under her armpits, and lifted her. She came up and cried out as she stood on her legs. He was able to get his mother into bed and then fed her soup out of the pot on the stove.

Thaddeus went to the shed and retrieved his bag and the other items he needed. He returned to his mother's room, sat on the bed, and took her hand into his.

"Mama, I'm going to leave tonight. I've had all of Ludwig that I'm going to take. I have my things in the living room and when I get settled, I'll send for you. I love you, and you will always be in my heart until I see you again." He leaned down and kissed her on the cheek, wiping the tears as they dropped off her cheek onto the bed.

"I love you, too, baby."

Thaddeus walked out of the house and headed to the river. When he arrived, he put all his supplies into the boat and put the gun in the back of the waistband of his pants. The walk to the tavern seemed to take a week, but was only a few minutes. He had something to say to his sorry of a man stepfather before he left Wichita.

Music could be heard as the hesitant young man slowed so he could look in the window of the tavern.

Men were drinking at tables, and a few bellied up to the bar. Three card tables were in the room, and he suspected Ludwig was sitting at the first table. That's what he did most nights, but the man wasn't visible from where Thaddeus stood at the window.

The inside of the tavern was well-lit, but the cigarette and cigar smoke created a fog. Ludwig was at one of the first poker tables, and evidently, he was having a good night, as shown by the stack of money in front of him.

Thaddeus took two steps inside the room, and his stepfather looked up and asked, "What do you want, runt?"

"I came in to tell you that you've beat my mother for the last time." Thaddeus reached behind his back and pulled the pistol out, pointed it at Ludwig, and then took one more step and hung his toe on a chair leg. Thaddeus started to the floor, and as he did, the gun fired. The noise was deafening in the room, and men rushed to get out of the way as Ludwig's head exploded. Pieces of skull, blood, and brain matter splattered the men on Ludwig's right side. The young man recovered his balance and, with tears streaming down his cheeks, he pointed the gun around the room and said, "If any of you want to try your luck with me tonight, then I'll kill you also. He almost beat my mother to death earlier today, and I'm glad he's dead."

Thaddeus walked to the table, reached down, took the stack of money, and then backed up toward the door. He stopped and turned the gun toward the man who worked as the bartender. "This tavern belongs to my mother now, and you better make sure no money comes up missing, or I'll come back for you." He then continued walking backward until he was outside on the wooden sidewalk. Anxiety set in, and he made a mad dash down the street for a block and then slowed to a walk until he could turn west toward the river, where the boat was waiting for his escape.

Less than ten minutes later, he was pushing the boat out onto the water.

Chapter Three

THADDEUS HAD ONLY BEEN ON THE ARKANSAS River a few times in his life, and maneuvering the boat in the direction he wanted it to go was a challenge for the young man. He hurriedly pushed the boat off the bank and immediately began to paddle, only to go in a counterclockwise circle. The current, along with him applying energy to one side of the boat, caused it to turn round and round.

The boy, Thaddeus, became so anxious to get away that his hands shook, and his breathing became difficult. The weight of his recent actions and the uncertainty of his future weighed heavily on him. "What am I doing wrong?" he asked. He stopped, closed his eyes, and settled down before blowing out a huge breath.

He needed to think. *If the boat turns when the paddle is exercised on one side, what will happen if I alternate sides? Wouldn't the boat go straight then?*

With a hard stroke to the right side of the boat, and then two strokes on the left side, the boat floated downstream. The faster he worked, the faster the boat went.

He also figured out that once the watercraft was heading downstream, he could rest and only make a few strokes with the paddle to keep it moving.

He began to think about his mother and all the pain she had endured these last few years. Ellen had transformed from a cheerful, kind, considerate lady to a beat-down woman who walked with her head down so people wouldn't see the bruises and scars on her once beautiful face. He didn't want to kill Ludwig, but that was the only way his sweet mother would ever be able to enjoy life.

Thaddeus thought about what she would do now that her husband was dead. Would she continue to operate the tavern or sell it? Either way, she would have money to buy the necessities to survive. The young son couldn't bear the thought of her being alone, but he knew he had to focus on his own survival for now.

It was getting dark, and Thaddeus thought about what he would do tonight. He could stay on the water and get as far away as possible before he rested or docked on the bank and make camp. Making camp sounded good since he didn't eat supper. Then it hit him. There wasn't any means to start a fire because, in the haste of things, lucifers weren't on the list. A great lesson was learned in planning, and he would have to get better to survive in the wild by himself.

What was he going to do? First, he would continue down the river, and if needed, sleep in the boat. When the river skirted through a settlement tomorrow, he would take the boat ashore and buy supplies. But what would he buy? Lucifers were the most critical item and maybe a small shovel to dig red worms for fishing. More bacon and a few more canned food items would come in handy. A man on the run had to be self-sufficient, living off the land and the river.

That sounded like a plan, and it was beginning to cool off with the darkness. The moon was out and gave a glistening light on the water. All kinds of different noises could be heard in the still of the night. There was the sound of crickets rubbing their front wings together. Bullfrogs could be heard croaking along the banks. A bird of some sort was making a shirking noise.

Thaddeus also needed to add a hunting rifle to his list of supplies. With the pistol used to kill Ludwig, shooting game would be almost impossible at any distance.

The words of Dr. Melrose came to him about a name change. If someone asked who he was, there was no way the young man could tell them the truth. The law was most likely looking for him now, and there could even be wanted posters with his picture on them hanging up in towns all over Kansas.

What would the new name be? He could change his last name to James. No, he couldn't use James because someone might try to associate him with the famous James gang that he had read about in the dime novels. He would come up with a last name that was common and one that wouldn't bring attention to him whenever he introduced himself to anyone.

Suddenly, something slapped him in the face, and then another. His face hurt and stung from the unexpected lick. Paddling as hard as he could on the right side of the boat took him back toward the middle of the stream. The boat had drifted too close to the north bank, where trees hung over the water, and that's what was slapping him in the face.

With the moon overhead, Thaddeus began to have second thoughts about leaving his mother to deal with the death of Ludwig and running the tavern. It would take time to get over missing the most important person in his life. But this was the best thing for him as he thought about his situation. A new life in a new town where he could work with a doctor would be ideal and then his mama could join him.

The thought of working for a doctor saddened him since becoming a doctor was out of the picture for now, unless he could buy books and continue to study. The young man had read stories of western doctors who had no formal education. Maybe he could become one of those in another state.

Sometime after midnight, the tired young man was so exhausted that he lay in the bottom of the boat and slept. The boat drifted by the current for a ways until it became lodged on a sandbar.

The sun, rising big and bright, cast its light onto the sleeping face, and Thaddeus woke up wondering where he was.

It took a few seconds to remember what had transpired yesterday in Wichita and why he was in the boat. Hunger pains gripped his empty stomach as he composed himself and looked at the surroundings. It looked like a safe place where his boat was moored on the sandbar. Using the knife from his bag to open one can of beans and sitting against the side of the boat, Thaddeus ate breakfast. Cold beans for breakfast wasn't the food he desired, but they tasted mighty good to the strapping young man.

With the beans in his stomach, it was time to go down the river. Taking the paddle to push the boat off the sand was to no avail. The boat was lodged on the sandbar and wouldn't move. Assessing the situation, he realized that the heavy wooden watercraft would need him out on land to put more force into shoving it free. The only shoes the boy had were lace-up Brogan boots, and he didn't want to get them wet, so he pulled off his boots and socks. The socks were beginning to stink, so he leaned over the edge of the boat and washed them out. He then wrung the water out and laid them where the sun would dry the material.

Not wanting to get his pants wet, he rolled up his britches legs, climbed out the front of the boat, and scared a water snake who was sunning at the front of the boat. The serpent took off, wiggling its way into the water, and Thaddeus stood there, almost wetting his pants. He would have to be more careful in the future. The next time, the snake may not shimmy off and decide to bite.

With the boat dislodged, he got it moving downstream in hopes of finding a town soon.

At first, he tried to stay on the side of the river where the trees shaded parts of the stream, but the mosquitoes were eating at him, so he crossed to the sunny side. The river was heading south to southeast, and he knew he had to be getting close to the town of El Paso, Kansas, soon.

Chapter Four

THE SUN WAS DIRECTLY OVERHEAD WHEN HE heard noises up ahead and figured he was getting close to El Paso, Kansas, which was eleven miles south of Wichita. It was the sound of a hammer hitting something made of steel. A woman called out loudly for someone called Hack, most likely a mother calling for her son.

The river skirted the town, and it was likely a short distance walk from the river once the boat was tied against the bank. The boat rounded a slight bend in the river, and there were two boats tied against the river-bank. Someone had fishing lines on long sticks stuck into the soil along the shoreline.

Thaddeus maneuvered his boat to shore, jumped out, and tied it so it wouldn't drift off with the current. He stood looking all around before getting back into the boat and retrieving his gun and holster. While doing so, Thaddeus saw an empty bean can, and inside were more fishing hooks, sinkers, and lines. Not sure how much money he had because there hadn't been time to count what he took the day he killed Ludwig. With the money laid out on one of the boat seats, the young man had a total of four hundred and eleven dollars.

Thaddeus started up a trail that the locals used to get down to the water, and when he was above the riverbed, it was time to have another look around and get a lay of the place. Nothing stuck out to the nervous lad as he walked toward the town a quarter of a mile away.

The blond-haired boy didn't know what to expect in the way of the law. Was he already a wanted man, and everyone was on the hunt for a cold-blooded killer. No, he wasn't like that. He wanted to help people, and that's the reason he wanted to be a doctor.

Frightened and afraid, the timid boy had killed in self-defense because if he hadn't, Ludwig would have eventually killed his mother and maybe him.

El Paso had been formed on Spring Creek before it dumped into the Arkansas River. The small town of less than three hundred people was getting ready for the railroad to come through, and businesses were already putting signs on their buildings welcoming rail workers and travelers.

Thaddeus saw Brody's Mercantile, Mrs. Mary's Café, and the Corner Grocery, and when he started toward the mercantile, three boys around the age of sixteen came from between two buildings and asked, "Who are you, and where did you come from?"

The boys spread out between Thaddeus and the store. Thaddeus put his hand on the butt of his pistol and said, "You boys need to move out of my way. I don't want any trouble, but I ain't afraid to hurt the three of you."

The three boys begin to laugh. "We just want to know your name. We mean you no harm."

Thaddeus looked past the boys, trying to find a name on one of the buildings he could use, when he said, "My name is Brody," and then he said, "It's Brody Connor, and then he lied. My folks are building a house two miles up the river."

The spokesman for the group said, "I'm Sammy," and pointed to his right. "This is Dan, and the ugly one is Isaiah. You have any money on you?"

Thaddeus shook his head. "Nope, I ain't got any money."

Dan stepped forward. "You're a liar. No one sends their kid to the store without money. I think I want to see what you got in your pockets."

Thaddeus came up with a right that landed on the boy's chin, and Dan dropped to the ground unmoving. "No one's taking my money. Is that clear?" said Thaddeus, standing in a fighter's stance with his fist ready, waiting on the other two.

Isaiah kneeled down and shook his friend, trying to get him up, when Sammy said, "You got a good right. We were only messing with you."

"I was only funning him also. I could have knocked all three of you out," said Thaddeus, standing with his hand on his gun.

As Sam and Isaiah helped Dan off down the street, Thaddeus smiled, or rather, Brody Connor. The last name was his real pa's first name. From now on, he would be called Brody Connor.

Brody was able to purchase the lucifers and a water-tight pouch to keep them dry, as well as a small shovel. He left the mercantile and headed to the grocery store, where he bought three pounds of bacon, a few potatoes, and salt. His last stop was at Homer's Gun Shop. There, he bought a .44 caliber, used Henry repeating rifle, and two boxes of shells for forty dollars. He placed all the smaller items, including the short-handle shovel, into a burlap sack and carried it with his right hand and the rifle in his left hand, returning to his boat.

With a good supply of provisions, the young man stowed his things and loaded the rifle with its fifteen-shell magazine. Brody started downstream. A half mile from where he had left his boat, Spring Creek ran into the Arkansas River. One of the fishing poles stuck in the bank was jerking up and down. There had to be a good-sized fish on it, and if no one was around, he would take it for supper. He looked all around and headed toward the pole. Sure enough, a four-pound catfish was on the line and Brody was removing the hook when he heard someone farther up the river hollering. An old man was waving his arms and cursing at him for stealing his fish.

Brody dropped the fish in the bottom of the boat and started to paddle as fast as he could. He didn't know what else to do, and his mouth was already watering, thinking how good a supper of fried fish would be tonight. Suddenly, the sound of a rifle being shot was heard, and water splashed behind him where the bullet landed. Frightened about getting shot, the boy paddled with all his might and another splash and another. By then, the lead shots were falling short of his boat, but the young man paddled as hard as he could to escape.

The river turned, and he could stop working so hard when the boat was around the bend. The streambed kept making turns through the flat land covered with trees on both sides of the watercourse. Brody put a fishing line through the fish's gill and put it into the water. With the line tied to the boat, the fish would stay alive until it was· time to be cleaned for supper.

Brody wanted to get as far away as possible, and as far as he knew, there wasn't another town for another twenty-five miles. His arms were sore from all the hard work, but he couldn't stop paddling the boat until he crossed the Kansas border into Indian Territory at Arkansas City.

As the sun started settling to the west, Brody began to look for a suitable location to make camp where he could have a fire and eat the stolen catfish.

The mosquitoes had been eating on him since he left Wichita, and it was a good thing he had on a long-sleeve shirt. On the hunt for a place to camp, the boy devised an idea to keep the pesky insects off. He would take mud and cover his exposed skin so the little blood suckers wouldn't have anything to attach to.

Brody eased the boat against the bank and began to get mud in his hands, which he applied to his neck, back of his head, face, and hands. With all the exposed skin covered, he took back off, and sure enough, none of the mosquitoes landed on him.

———

RIGHT AT DUSK, a herd of cattle was drinking water from the river. Brody quit paddling until the cows were filled with water and left. This would be where his camp would be for the night.

With only his rifle, he climbed out of the boat and followed the cattle trail up to flat land. It was a good place to have his camp, with abundant wood for his fire. Before unloading the supplies, he gathered enough firewood to last all night and then carried only the items he would need from the boat.

It took a few minutes to start the campfire and even longer to clean the fish. Fish and potatoes filled the hungry lad, who was so tired that he laid out his bedroll and went to sleep.

———

SOMETIME BEFORE DAYLIGHT, he heard something walking close to where he lay. He raised up with the pistol and could only see a significant dark figure moving around his camp.

"Get out of here," he yelled and jumped up, frightening the three cows that were close by. "Stupid cows," said the boy, putting more wood on his fire.

Still tired from a hard day on the river, he took a swallow of water and lay back down. As the sun was coming up, Brody opened his eyes and then shielded them with his arm. He had to get started but took the time to cook bacon before he loaded up his gear.

Chapter Five

BY THAT AFTERNOON, THE HEAT AND HUMIDITY
had soaked Brody's clothes, and he had drank all the
water from his canteen. He would need fresh water soon,
or he would be dehydrated by nightfall. Getting to the
state line was his priority, but he needed to protect his
health while doing so.

It was getting close to four in the afternoon by the
sun's position, and the heat hadn't let up. He had seen
a few places where water had seeped from the river-
banks into the stream. With the hopes of finding water
from a spring, the boy continued on. As he came
around a bend in the river, smoke could be seen up on
the bank, and that meant someone was camped up
there.

A decision had to be made quickly. Should the boy
continue on or see if whoever was up there would share
their campsite for the night? The camp could be by fresh
water, and hopefully they would share their food and talk
to the lonely lad. Although he was apprehensive about
going up the bank to the camp, he docked his boat, put

the pistol into the back of his britches, and carried his rifle.

"Hello in the camp. Can I come up and join you?" asked Brody.

"Come on up, we're friendly," called out someone that the boy couldn't see.

He made his way up the riverbank, only sliding a few times up the steep embankment to encounter three grizzly-looking men standing a few feet away from the fire where a skillet was simmering with meat being cooked.

"I'm headed down the river and saw the smoke from your fire and thought you might have fresh water up here," said Brody.

All three men started laughing, and Brody didn't know what he said that was so funny.

"Did I say something funny?" asked the boy.

All three men had long hair and dirty long beards, and some of their last couple of meals were still stuck to the facial hair and the front of their nasty shirts. Their britches were also filthy, and he could tell by the smell that none of them had bathed in weeks.

One of the men stopped laughing and pointed a dirty finger with a long, nasty nail toward the river. "There's a whole river full of fresh water. We can tell by your looks that you're a tenderfoot city slicker out here and dumber than a gourd."

Brody pointed to the river water. "I don't drink out of some dirty river."

One of the men tilted his head sideways to get a better look at the visitor. "Boy, why is your face and head covered in mud?"

"It keeps the mosquitoes off me."

Another of the men took a couple of steps toward the boy and brought up his gun and pointed it at the muddied young man. "Hand over that rifle and empty your pockets before we throw you back down into the river tied to a rock."

A strange feeling hit Brody in the pit of his stomach, and he felt like he was being pushed into doing something he had no control over. This man would not take his gun or money today or any day. He might be a city slicker, but he would fight when backed into a corner, and this was his corner.

Brody shifted the rifle to his left hand and held the gun out, where the man had to take a couple of steps to get it. As the man walked toward him with his eyes on the new rifle, Brody reached his right hand behind his back and took hold of the pistol, and cocked the hammer back.

"Here you go," said the boy, and pitched the rifle toward the approaching man. He pulled the pistol from behind him, pointed it at the man's left thigh, and pulled the trigger. The man stumbled backward, dropped his gun, and grabbed his thigh. He looked up at Brody and said, "You shot me!"

The injured man's knee buckled, and he went to the ground, hollering out in pain. Brody turned the gun toward the other two men and shifted his eyes to the man on the ground. "I'm sorry that I had to shoot you, mister, but I'm not afraid to kill when I have to."

Brody turned his attention to the other men. "You two throw your guns over there and lie on your stomachs."

With the two men disarmed and on the ground. Brody picked up his rifle and hit one of the men in the back of his head, but all it did was make the man cry out in pain and try to get up. The scared boy put a foot in the man's back and shoved him back down.

"I'm sorry I hurt you. I thought the blow would knock you out. Don't move, or I'll hit you again." Brody kicked the gun away from the man he shot. The boy could see blood seeping out of the nasty man's thigh and knew that he had to help with the bullet wound. "Hold your hand over the hole while I find something to tie up your partners."

"We ain't going to try anything," said one of the men on his stomach.

Brody noticed that one of the men had on lace-up boots. "You on the right, take the laces out of your boots."

The man on the left looked down at his boots. "I don't have bootstraps."

Brody shifted the gun toward the man. "Do you not know your left from right? I was talking to the man on my right. Now take out the boot strings and use one to tie up your partner."

When the man was tied, Brody tied up the other man's hands and went back to the feller he shot.

The man had a long blade knife in a sheath attached to his belt. Brody pulled out the knife and put the tip into the wound, and the man cried out in pain and went limp from passing out. With a bit of digging, he extracted the bullet and held his hand on the bullet hole until he could come up with a way to stop the bleeding.

The meat was sizzling in the skillet, and a new plan came into place. Brody put the knife blade into the fire, and after a minute or so, the blade was glowing red. He quickly removed his hand from the wound and applied the red-hot blade to the bloody skin. Smoke and burning flesh filled his nostrils with an awful smell, but the bleeding stopped.

The man was still alive but would most likely have an

infection from the lack of disinfectant and the filth from his body. Brody went to the other two men, grabbed them by their arms, and dragged them away from the campfire another four feet so they wouldn't get too hot. "Thanks for moving us. Is Lucky going to be all right?"

"Yeah, I think so," said Brody. "He'll have to keep the wound clean, or it'll get infected."

The other two men laughed. "Ole Lucky has enough dirt on him to ward off any infection that comes knocking."

Brody walked away from their campfire to see if they had horses. With horses, he could get to the Indian Territory border faster, but it looked like they didn't have any. He returned to the fire and asked, "Where are your horses?"

"We ain't got no horses," said one of the men.

Brody kneeled by the fire so he could look at the meat in the skillet. It was done, and he took it off the fire and set the skillet to the side to cool. Before eating, he went back to the boat, filled his only pot with river water, and returned to the camp. The water would boil for fifteen minutes and then cool enough to be poured into the canteen. Dr. Melrose had taught the young man how to boil water to make it sterile and safe to drink.

The meat in the skillet was delicious, and he cut it into bite-sized chunks so that he could feed a little to the two men tied up. He saved a few pieces for the hurt man when he woke up. Brody had laid out his bedroll and would sleep here tonight to have the fire's light.

The man he removed the bullet from started moaning sometime during the night, and when Brody came awake, the man was trying to sit up. "Lay back down. If you move around, the wound will open up, and you'll bleed to death. I'll get you some water, and I saved you a little of the meat to eat."

Brody had filled his canteen with purified water, and now that the man was awake, he put another pot on to boil to refill his canteen.

After feeding and giving the hurt man water, Brody lay on his bedroll, looking up at the stars and thought about what had happened. He could have killed these three men, and it would have been justified since they had tried to steal his gun and money. He knew that taking a life was a big deal, and he was glad the situation hadn't escalated to more than one man getting hurt. In the morning, he would leave, and the man he shot could untie his friends after he was gone.

Chapter Six

THE FOLLOWING MORNING, BRODY GATHERED his things and said, "I'm leaving now. Your injured friend can untie you when I'm gone."

With his gear stowed away inside the boat and back navigating the river current, the three men could be heard talking loudly as the young man continued down the river heading to Oxford, Kansas. He estimated that it would be sometime tomorrow before he would arrive.

Brody stopped long enough in a couple of miles to dig worms and bait out two fishing poles on the back of the boat once he was back floating down the stream. Occasionally, he would catch a fish and put it on a stringer for supper.

Late that afternoon, a good stopping place came into view where the riverbank sloped upward to a grove of pecan trees. Squirrels could be seen running and jumping from limb to limb. The boy thought about shooting a few for supper, but by the time he had camp set up, both the fishing poles had a fish on them to add to what he had, and that would be good eating tonight.

As Brody lay on his bedroll that night, he kept wondering why he didn't feel bad about killing Ludwig and shooting the man on the river. Did he not care that he took a life and hurt another man, or did he care more about his survival? Whatever the reason, it most likely would happen again since he was now on the run and in unfamiliar surroundings.

Brody knew that whatever he did and wherever he settled down, it would be up to him to carve out his future. Being alone out here would require him to learn how to stay alive.

———

THE NEXT DAY, in the early afternoon, he found where the Ninnescah River merged with the Arkansas River. Oxford couldn't be more than a few miles farther south. Brody paddled his boat to shore at the first sandbar and took off his clothes to bathe and wash off the mud that protected him from the mosquitoes. First, he washed his clothes, hung them to dry, and then washed off all the mud. The water felt good, and when he finished bathing, Brody put on the only change of clean clothing he had brought with him. His other clothes were still wet, so he spread them out in the boat.

Thirty minutes or so later, going down the river, Brody could hear noises up ahead and was on alert when he saw the bridge that crossed the Arkansas River. Then he saw the raceway where water was diverted into a large two-story stone building, and a sign on the structure read, *Oxford Best Products*. He didn't know what that was but assumed it was some sort of manufacturing plant since a large water wheel was gathering water and supplying it to the massive building.

The Oxford area was initially settled by the Osage Indians until the government moved them south into the northeastern Indian Territory. The rich farmland around Oxford was given to settlers from the north. Graff's store was one of the first businesses, and even a printing press was shipped in. The Donley and McMillan sawmills provided lumber for folks who were building houses in the early days.

The entire town fought for the Confederate army during the Civil War. The few residents that didn't fight moved south, and the town became housing for Union soldiers. After the war, most of the houses and businesses were in shambles and had to be rebuilt.

Brody tied up his boat and strapped on the holster with the pistol. He hid his rifle under a fallen tree and started into town. The two-story rock schoolhouse was the next largest building that could be seen. The young man marveled at all the town stores and thought about why he was even here. Stakes were driven into the ground all along the west side of the town. A sign finally told him the story of why they were there. It was the future route of the Crowley, Sumner & Fort Smith Railroad.

The front of the large building on the banks of the river was indeed a manufacturing plant. Oxford Best Products was a flour mill that processed wheat grown in the southern part of Kansas. The railroad extended its line to ship the flour to eastern markets.

Brody decided to eat a good meal at the town's café before he did anything else and started down the dirt street. Only a few people were in town at that time of day, and no one paid any attention to him. They probably saw a lot of strangers in the town, especially young men working for the future railroad coming through. This was a farming community, and the need to ship grain to other markets was increasing every year. It wasn't uncommon to see a farmhand with a shotgun or rifle, but today was different. The young man walking down the street was a stranger dressed in city clothes and wearing a sidearm.

Brody continued on toward the café, and as he passed by the Oxford Independent News Paper, the edition nailed to the wall of the business caught his attention. The headlines read, *Killer on the loose*. The article told how a young man by the name of Thaddeus Malloy walked into the German Tavern and murdered his father, Ludwig Muller. It described a young man with long blonde hair, a brown shirt, and gray and black tweed britches.

Brody looked around to make sure no one was paying much attention to him and continued toward the café. The poster caused the young man to be concerned about someone recognizing him from the description. The news was out, and likely every town that had a news-paper or telegraph knew about him killing Ludwig. He needed to eat, buy new clothes, and get rid of the clothes he had drying in the boat. If the three men he had the run-in with on the river were found, the author-ities would suspect it was him and be on the manhunt soon, and Oxford could be the next place the law looked.

At that time of day, the café only had a few patrons eating, and Brody ate his fill of food while thinking about his next move. Buying new clothes was necessary, but he would also go to the barber shop and have his hair cut short.

Walking to the barber shop made him keep an eye on each side of the street. Farther down the dirt road was a livery stable advertising that it sold horses. While he was in the barber chair, the man cutting his hair said, "Mister, you should wear a hat more often. Going without a hat causes the sun to bleach out your hair."

"Is that the reason it's so yellow?"

"Yep, I would bet if you wore a hat, it would be almost brown when it grows back out," replied the barber.

Brody changed the subject. "Do you know how much a good horse costs?"

"Man ought to pay around a hundred dollars for a good solid pony."

"I'm going to buy a riding horse when we make enough money," said Brody, dropping the conversation.

After paying the barber for the haircut, he walked to the livery stable, where he found a man out back working with horses. The hostler had a rope on the horse's neck, and the animal walked in a circle.

Brody walked up to the rail fence. "Howdy, are you the livery man?"

"Yep, I'm Amos. Who might you be?"

"I'm Brody Connor, and I saw where you have horses for sale. How much do you want for a good riding horse, saddle, and bridle?"

Amos walked to the gate. "Come with me, and I'll show you what I have."

Brody followed the man to another pen where five horses were eating hay. "That chestnut over there is my best horse for one hundred thirty dollars."

Brody had his eyes on a gray gelding. "How much for the gray horse?"

"I can sell that one for one hundred fifteen dollars."

Brody made a face when he heard the price. "That's a lot of money. How much for the gray with a saddle, blanket, and bridle?"

"I have a really nice Mexican-style saddle and bridle

that I can throw in for one hundred fifty-five," said Amos.

Brody walked where he could see the horse better and kicked dried manure out of his way. He turned to Amos and shook his head. "That's too rich for my blood. I reckon that I'll have to pass on it."

"How much do you have to spend on a horse?" asked Amos.

"We just moved here, and all we have is one hundred and forty dollars. I guess I should be going," said Brody and started off.

Amos reached out and took hold of the boy's arm. "Hold on now. Being you're new in these parts, I reckon I could sell you that gray and the riding gear for what you have, but don't go blabbing that I came down on my price around town. That could hurt my business."

Brody held out his hand to seal the deal. "Thank you, sir, I appreciate it."

"If you have a few more things to do in town, go ahead and do them while I fetch the gray and saddle him up for you."

"Yes, sir, I'll be back in a few minutes."

Chapter Seven

On the way to the dry goods store, a door opened, and a man came out carrying a black bag like the one that Dr. Melrose used when making a house call. Brody waited until the man turned at the end of the block before he went back to read the sign beside the door: *Dr. P A Wood*, was painted on a board.

Brody, in the midst of trying on boots in the dry goods store, had a sudden stroke of resourcefulness. He hadn't seen the doctor lock his door when he left, and with the boy already in trouble with the law, what would it hurt to venture inside the doctor's office and see if he had any medical books that he could take with him.

Wearing a new pair of riding boots and a hat on his head, the boy carried his bag with a pair of britches, a shirt, and a coat. Brody entered the doctor's office and called out, "Hello, is anyone here?"

There was no answer, so it was time to see what he could find in the way of medical books. There were no books in the first two rooms, but books were stacked on a table in what looked like an office. Three books were in a stack from the University of Pennsylvania that he wanted. They were Anatomy, Surgery, and Bandaging. He carefully untied his package and placed the books where they wouldn't show or fall out, and at the door, he cracked it open to make sure no one was on the boardwalk that could see him.

Brody walked at normal speed to the livery, where the gray horse was tied in front of the stable. Amos saw him coming and walked to the horse.

"Your horse is ready to go, and all you have to do is pay me, and you can be on your way."

Brody counted out the money and handed it to the man. "I sure do appreciate you helping me out."

Amos pointed to a short piece of rope hanging from the saddle. "That rope with the loops on each end is used as a hobble so the horse doesn't wander off at night. Have you ever used hobbles before?"

"No, sir."

Amos took the rope and showed the boy how to put it on the horse's front legs. When he was through, the liveryman lowered his voice and said, "You be sure and give him plenty of water and rest along your journey. Now let me hold your package while you mount up."

"Thanks, Mr. Amos, I'll do my best to care for him." Brody had only ridden a horse on two occasions until today. He tried hard not to screw up, and when he was in the saddle, Amos handed him his things. "Good luck out there. The state line is due south, about thirty miles away. You may want to spend the night at Slate Creek."

The boy knew that Amos had identified who he was and had helped him in a great way. He turned the horse, and off he went toward the river.

The boat was still where he had left it earlier, and it looked as if no one had been at that particular location in his absence. It didn't take long to realize that there were more items to take with him than he had room for.

Brody carefully considered his needs, and a plan began to form in his mind. He could carry the book and some of his supplies if there were saddlebags. He had one burlap sack and another bag could hold the rest of his things. The other essential item was a saddle scabbard for his rifle. Without one, he would always have to carry it in his hands.

With the supplies hidden by a tree higher up the embankment, the boy pushed the boat off the bank and watched it drift with the current. The hope was that it would drift away from Oxford before anyone found it.

Brody rode back into town and tied his horse close to the saloon, where four horses stood at the hitching rail. He eyed the gear on the four horses on his way back to the café for supper, hoping it would get dark soon.

After supper, the boy walked to the gun shop and asked the man, "Sir, would you happen to have a used rifle scabbard for a saddle?"

"I have two of 'um. They're over here," said the man, walking to the far wall and removing the scabbards. "What kind of rifle do you have?"

"It's a Henry repeating rifle," said Brody, eyeing them over.

The store owner pointed to one with multiple scuffs on the leather. "I'll take three dollars for either one? I think this one will be a better fit for the Henry."

"How does it attach to the saddle?" asked Brody.

"If you'll bring your horse by here, I can show you," said the shop owner.

"I'll take it. Thank you, sir. I'll go get my horse and bring him here," said Brody, taking off.

In a few minutes, the kind man showed the boy how

to attach it to the saddle, and then he had Brody get astride the horse so he could make the final adjustments. When the store man was finished, the happy young man thanked the store owner a second time before he rode to the mercantile.

Inside the store, he found a bag he could buy for a dollar. It was large enough to carry the rest of his supplies. The darkness began taking over the street when he returned to the saloon and dismounted. Down the street, someone was lighting streetlamps, but it was dark where he was, and that was the ideal time for the boy to make his move.

Dismounting on the offside, he untied the straps that secured the saddlebags on the horse beside him. With one swift move, he removed the bags and placed them behind the cantle on the back of his horse. He didn't take the time to tie the straps that would secure the bags, and got back into the saddle. His horse walked down the street with Brody holding the reins in one hand and the other holding onto the saddlebags.

Thirty minutes later, the boy had all his gear tucked away and was heading south from Oxford. To his surprise, he found another gun, six dollars, a coffee cup, and two handkerchiefs in the saddlebags. All those items would come in handy down the road, adding an unexpected twist to his journey.

Not being a skilled rider, he let the horse go where he wanted, and Brody kept getting hit in the face and body by low branches. He finally realized the horse wasn't looking up to see what would interfere with the rider. In one instance, the limb almost took the boy from the saddle. The only saving grace was that the animal was walking, and Brody could stop him from going forward.

This was a learning experience, and the tenderfoot

rider had better learn quickly or he'd hit the ground hard.

Brody rode until after the moon was past midnight. He didn't want some drunk cowboy coming after him tonight looking for his saddlebags. The camp was without fire that night, and as he lay staring up at the sky, he told himself, *my mind needs to shut up so I can get some sleep.*

Chapter Eight

THE SUN WAS ALREADY UP WHEN THE LONE traveler woke up under a cottonwood tree. The wind blowing through the leaves was making a sound like water cascading over rocks. He lay on his bedroll and marveled at how far he had come and was still a free man. The future was something that would come about by the grace of God and clear thinking on his part.

The horse was some sixty feet away, eating grass. Brody shook out his boots before putting them on, and a scorpion fell out. He had never done that before, but he was sure glad he did today. That was something he would make a habit of doing in the future.

He noticed a creek up ahead while gathering sticks to make a small fire to fry bacon. Amos had told him that a good place to stop would be Slate Creek, and this may be the location. With it so close and his horse needing water, he went ahead and rolled up his bedroll and then went after the horse.

Getting the saddle on the back of the gray took him a couple of tries, but he finally managed and secured his belongings. The horse was easy to lead to the stream, where it filled up on water. Brody's butt and thighs were so sore from riding that he walked gingerly all the way to the creek.

The canteen was empty, but the traveler was afraid to use the creek water. This wasn't the time or place to get sick out in the middle of nowhere. He went ahead and built a fire large enough to boil water and fry bacon for breakfast. Although it delayed him a good thirty minutes, it was well worth the effort to drink good water, and the hunger pains subsided.

Three hours and many miles later, he rode up on four covered wagons heading in a southwest direction. The wagons must have been loaded heavily because of the oxen straining against the yoke attached to the wagon tongue. There were two of the colossal beasts pulling each wagon. The lead wagon had a man with a cane walking beside the oxen. The second wagon had women in dresses and bonnets tending to the large animals. The third one had a young man younger than Brody walking with the oxen. Each one carried a cane or switch to keep the oxen moving forward.

The last wagon had two huge workhorses attached to the tongue, and in the seat was another man, but younger than the man in the lead.

Brody rode off to the side of the small caravan and noticed that no one had on a sidearm. When he was even with the leader of the first wagon, he removed his hat and waved it in the air. "Hello, may I come talk to you, mister?"

The man turned his head and spoke to someone in the wagon. A rifle barrel came out of the front opening, and the man called out, "Come on in, but keep those hands where we can see them."

Brody rode in and said, "I'm Brody Connor. Do you happen to know where we're at?"

"Yep, we're in Indian Territory. I reckon you came down from Kansas," said the man.

Brody shook his head up and down. "That's right. I left home in Kansas and headed out to make my own way. Do you mind if I ride along with you folks for aways? It gets mighty lonely out here by myself."

"I reckon you can. I'm Robert Mosley, and you can call me Bob. Iffin, you plan on sharing our food tonight, you'll have to contribute to the meal."

"I sure would like to eat and sleep close by tonight, but I'm not sure how you want me to contribute to the meal," said Brody.

"You have a horse and a rifle. Go kill a deer or a young buffalo, and that will be plenty," said Bob.

"I assume you'll stay on the same trajectory that you're headed for the rest of the day," said Brody.

The man looked at the boy briefly and said, "I'm not sure what trajectory means."

"Are you going to be heading in the same direction as you are now?" asked Brody.

"Yep. We're staying in this direction until we come to the Chisholm Trail. When we find it, we'll head south into Texas and then head for Fort Worth," said Bob.

"I'll go on ahead and see if I can kill us something for supper tonight," said Brody, and took off. He didn't look back until he was almost out of sight and figured those folks were getting low on food if they needed him to kill a deer.

It felt strange since he only saw those herding the oxen and the man driving the wagon. Evidently, there were more folks in the wagons. He was deep in thought when, out of the corner of his eyes, he saw two deer

43

feeding on wild blackberries. Brody stopped his horse and tied it to a branch while he took his rifle and eased closer to the does. When he was in a position to shoot, one of the deer raised its head, and that's when Brody held his breath and pulled the trigger. The deer jumped on all fours and then took off, and the other one went in the opposite direction. Brody was shocked that he had missed it, but he wanted to make sure and walked where they had been feeding. Splotches of blood were on the ground and on the leaves of the berries.

He returned to his horse and started to follow the bloody trail until it vanished. He sat in the saddle, began sweeping the area where the trail stopped, and saw his supper dead a few feet away.

He had never skinned a deer before but had seen them hung from a limb, but remembered they had all been gutted before they were brought in, to skin and process.

An hour later, the boy had the deer gutted and lying across his saddle as he walked on foot, leading his horse. The walk was less than a mile when he found the wagons on the bank of the Sharkaskee River. The two men, along with three boys and three women, were digging on the bank of the river, making a crossing for the wagons.

Brody rode up and said, "I have fresh meat for supper if someone knows how to skin it. I've never skinned one before, but I'm willing to learn if someone will show me."

Bob looked at the younger man using the shovel. "Lester, you go help Brody skin the deer, and we'll finish up here directly."

"Yes, sir, Pa," said Lester, taking his shovel to one of the wagons. He came to the horse and helped Brody remove the deer, and the two men took it over by a tree.

"Come with me, and I'll get what we need from the wagon, and by the way, I'm Lester."

Brody had dried blood all over his hands and the front of his shirt. He looked at his hand and said, "Sorry about the bloody hands, I'm Brody."

"That's all right, you'll have a lot more on them by the time we're through."

Chapter Nine

LESTER WAS A GOOD TEACHER, EXPLAINING HOW to cut down the back legs and remove the skin without getting hair all over the meat. By the time they had the deer skinned and the hams, front shoulders, and back strap removed, the others were ready to make camp where they were and cook up as much meat as they could.

The women and children gathered enough wood to have three fires. The men unloaded a table from the back of one wagon. The legs had been removed to save room during transit, but it didn't take long to get set up so the men could finish processing the meat.

Brody had so much fun learning how to use the knife and hone his skills so he could provide for himself in the future. Lester showed him how to cut out ligaments, tendons, and membranes, then slice the meat as thin as possible so the women could make jerky. It took everyone helping to get the meat sliced and cooking.

This was also the perfect time to meet everyone with the caravan. Robert's wife was named Susan. The other man was Lester, and his wife was named Violet, who was also pregnant and big as a barrel.

Bob and Susan had another son named Thomas, who was sixteen, and a thirteen-year-old daughter named Debbie. Lester and Violet had two smaller children, Sally, seven, and Willie, five.

Brody really liked the families, and after eating a meal of deer meat and potatoes, they all sat around the fire talking about where they were headed and their dreams of having their own places to farm and raise cattle. None of the men wore pistols, and Bob made it clear that they were all God-fearing people and didn't believe in carrying guns.

Brody kept watching Violet rub her stomach, and she would make a face like she was in pain every once in a while. He suspected that something was wrong with her facial display of discomfort, but he was hesitant to ask. Then, she got up and started to walk around the campsite.

Brody couldn't sit still any longer as he watched the young mother in pain. "Excuse me, Violet. You seem to be experiencing some discomfort with the baby. I have experience with childbirth. I was a doctor's assistant for two years and helped him deliver nine babies."

"I think it's getting close to coming out. The baby is kicking and moving all the time in there, and I'm so miserable carrying around all this weight."

Susan chimed in. "You need to let the Lord do his work with the child."

"That's well and good, but sometimes the Lord puts people in your path so they can help you," said Brody, and he had no idea where that came from since he had never been to church or read the Bible.

Bob pulled out a sack of tobacco and commenced to

fill his cheek. When he had a big bulge, he said, "You're absolutely right, young man, and we're grateful that the good Lord sent you our way with the fresh meat. I'm hoping that you can stay with us for a day or so until Violet delivers. My wife has helped birth a few youngins, but we may need all the help we can get with that baby as big as it is."

"I can stay as long as you need me," said Brody, and got up. He walked to where Violet stood and went down onto his knees. "Mrs. Violet, I'm going to listen to the baby, and then I'm going to feel around on your stomach."

The boy put his left ear against her stomach and would move it to a different location every few seconds. He put both hands on her stomach and felt around as he listened. "Everything sounds good. I can hear the baby's heartbeat, and he seems to be in the correct position. I believe you'll be giving birth in the next few days, and I don't want you lifting anything heavy or doing any strenuous work."

Violet nodded her head. "I've been watching what I do lately, Doctor."

"Just call me Brody. I ain't a full-fledged doctor yet, but I intend to become one someday."

Brody walked back to where the others were sitting and said, "Mrs. Susan, we'll need to sterilize some towels and bandages when the time comes to help Violet in delivery."

"I don't know what you mean by sterilizing towels and bandages," said Susan. "We ain't never done that before."

"We all have germs on us, and especially, on our hands. Everyone helping Violet give birth will need to scrub their hands with lye soap and dry them with sterilized towels. The way to kill germs is to boil water for at least fifteen minutes and then put the cloth in the boiling water for another fifteen minutes. We'll hang the material to dry, and it should be fine. By doing this, we cut down on the chance of Violet or the baby getting an infection," said Brody.

"Can we go ahead and sterilize everything we need and hang it in one of the wagons tonight?" asked Lester.

"Sure, and when it's dry, whoever folds it has to wash their hands first and then stow it in a trunk or case of some sort," said Brody.

Bob stood up and said, "Thomas, go fetch a couple of buckets, and I'll go to the river with you for water. Lester can stoke up the fires while Susan sets out the boiling pots and gathers up what you need."

An hour later, the material was being hung in one of the wagons for the night. Everyone was tired, and Brody moved away from the others to find a place to lay his bedroll. As he lay looking up at the stars, he couldn't help but wonder if, by some miracle, God had looked down on him and confirmed his purpose in life. Maybe Bob was right today when he said God had sent Brody here. That was such a confidence builder, and he had a comforting feeling knowing that Violet and her baby would be fine.

Chapter Ten

PEOPLE TALKING WOKE BRODY UP THE following morning. He had been exhausted the night before and was still sore from riding the horse. The sun was rising, and one of the travelers had already put wood on two fires. A large coffee pot and a pan of water were heating on one of the fires while two skillets were sitting on hot coals on the second fire.

Brody got up and rolled up his bedroll before going to where the others were sitting. He looked at Violet and asked, "How was your night?"

"It was fine. The baby woke me up a few times, but I got some rest."

"Coffee will be ready in a jiffy," said Bob.

"That's all right, I've never drank coffee before," said Brody.

"You may be the first person I've ever known who didn't drink coffee. We all have our morning cup with breakfast," said Bob, surprised by Brody's unique habit.

After a hearty breakfast of deer meat and fried bread, the men were bustling with the oxen, while the women efficiently stowed pots, pans, and eating utensils. Brody led his horse to where Bob and Lester were working and asked, "Is one set of oxen enough to pull the wagons across the river and up that far bank?"

Lester replied, "Pa thinks it is, but I'm not sure."

"Let's take the first one over, and we'll know if we need to take the time to use two teams," said Bob.

"It's not really none of my business how you do it, but do you know how deep the river is?" asked Brody.

"Not really, but I'm assuming it's not up to the wagon beds," said Bob.

"Would you like me to ride my horse across and see if I can find where it's the shallowest?" asked Brody, offering a practical solution to the potential problem of the river's depth.

"Pa, that's a good idea. We can't afford to get everything wet or lose a wagon in the river," said Lester.

"Fine, go ahead while we finish up with the yokes," said Bob.

Brody rode the gray across and back by a different location twice, moving upstream each time. When he rode back to where Bob and Lester were, he said, "We can cross the first two wagons here and then move over for the next two to cross. The river bottom is pretty boggy, and I'm afraid they'll get stuck if we cross all the wagons in one spot."

"I'll take my wagon across first, and then Brody can bring me back over to help with the next one said Lester."

Lester took the lighter of his two wagons across, and the oxen, despite their initial struggle, managed to reach the far bank. Their determination was palpable as they heaved the wagon up the muddy river embankment.

Brody rode over and up the bank to find Lester tying

his oxen to a tree. "I didn't think you would make it to the top," said Brody.

"We have to unhook this pair and use them to help with the other two wagons. There ain't no way a single pair can pull the heavier wagons through the river," said Lester and walked to the edge of the stream and called out. "Get the spare pole from under the wagon. I'm bringing this team back over, and they'll have to help with the crossing."

Brody dismounted and helped to unfasten the huge animals from the wooden tongue. Lester guided the oxen down the riverbank, and entered the stream, urging the steers back to where Bob and Thomas were waiting in the second wagon.

Bob had already fastened the extra pole, which had a steel ring on each end, to the ring of the wagon tongue. Lester arranged for his team to be in position, and Bob attached the yoke to the ring on the pole. Brody stood back, watched how the men worked together, and was amazed how they could hook more than one team of oxen to a wagon.

Brody dismounted and went to the last wagon, where Violet was lying on top of quilts that had been folded to make her a bed. "Mrs. Violet, how are you doing this morning?"

"I'm miserable, and this baby has been kicking all morning. I think he's about ready to come out," said Violet.

Brody looked behind him. "I'm going after Susan. I need her to look at you down there to see if you're beginning to get bigger."

With a confused look on her face. "Why can't you do that?"

This embarrassed the young man. "I think it would be better if she did that."

Bob and Lester were going up the far bank when he found Susan and told her what he wanted her to do. She checked on Violet, and her advice was for the men to take Violet over next in case the baby decided to come out.

Nothing happened, and with all four wagons across the river and the oxen yoked up to their wagons, Brody took the lead around eleven that morning, and the caravan headed out.

They traveled five miles before Bob called out, "Find us a good place to make camp. We've come far enough and need to rest our teams."

Brody found a small creek with enough water for camp use and to water the animals. He wanted to fill the pots before the oxen and horses went to fill up. The animals didn't know any better than to stand in the stream, and most of the time, they either peed or pooped, and it landed in the water.

When the first wagon arrived, the young man was waiting so he could fill the pots from the stream. By the time the last wagon stopped, he had filled four buckets with water and gathered up firewood. Bob, Lester, and Thomas took the animals to the creek before they were led to graze.

Bob came over to Brody after he had removed the saddle off his horse. "Brody, can I give you some advice?"

"Sure, Bob. What is it?"

"After you take the saddle off your horse, it's a good practice to grab a big handful of grass and wipe him down, especially where the saddle was. He's your only transportation, and you need to learn to care for him."

"I'm still new at this and didn't know that. I appreciate you giving me advice, and if you see anything else I need to be doing, please tell me."

Susan and Debbie fixed supper while Violet rubbed her stomach, sitting against one of the wagon wheels. Brody could tell that she was in a lot of discomfort, and as they were eating supper, she set down her plate and stood up. "Oh my goodness." Brody looked at her and knew it was time to start preparing for the arrival of a new life. Her water had broken and soaked the front of her dress and down to her bare feet.

Brody put his plate down and walked to Violet as she stood apologizing to the rest of the group. She thought she had peed and was embarrassed.

"Mrs. Violet, your water just broke, and the baby is getting ready to meet us. You stay here while we make you a bed on the ground," said Brody. He turned to the others and said, "Susan, you're in charge of making Violet a pallet on the ground and getting those sanitized towels out for me. Lester, get one of those buckets of water boiling and bring out some lanterns."

Brody went to the wash pan and filled it with fresh water before he scrubbed his hands. He walked back to where Lester and Bob were helping Violet to the pallet. "Susan, you need to remove that dress and cover her with a blanket. I also need you to check down there again to see if she has begun to expand."

Violet looked up at Brody and raised her hand for him to take. "Brody, it's all right. I trust you, and you can examine me." And then a pain hit her, and she screamed out.

Chapter Eleven

Two hours later, Brody kneeled beside Violet, holding the baby girl. He had just finished giving her a few swats on the hind end to get her crying and breathing on her own. "You have a beautiful little girl." The young man was grinning from ear to ear.

Susan came over with a towel and wet cloth and cleaned the baby while Brody held it. He then laid the tiny child on Violet's stomach and said, "Susan, I need sewing thread and a pair of scissors to cut the cord."

Susan, with her hands on her hips. "We always let it fall off in a few days."

Brody was tired and wasn't going to argue with the woman. "Please do as I ask, I know what I'm doing."

Susan looked at Bob, who motioned with his hand, and she walked to one of the wagons and returned with thread. "I have the thread and scissors."

"Good, where the cord stops pulsating, you can tie the string around it and then cut it loose. This is the way doctors do it now," said Brody.

Susan followed his directions, and then he had Susan

take care of Violet and clean her up as well. Brody went to the wash pan and scrubbed off the blood from his hands and arms. When he was finished, Debbie came to him and said, "Pa said if you want to change your clothes, I can wash them for you."

"I appreciate that, Debbie, but I think I'll wait a little while to make sure Violet and the baby are going to be fine. Plus, I can use a cup of that coffee about now."

"I didn't think you drank coffee," she replied.

"I didn't until now," said Brody, and started laughing. "This has been some night, wouldn't you say?"

"Yes, sir, I would. I reckon we need to start calling you Dr. B."

"Right now, I'm so tired that you can call me anything."

Debbie pointed to a log. "Go sit down, and I'll get you a cup of coffee with a little sugar to cut the bitter taste."

Brody watched as Lester sat with his wife, holding their new daughter. Violet looked at Brody and said, "I already had a name picked out to use. but I'm thinking about naming her Bonnie since that's pretty close to Brody, what do you think, Doctor?"

"I think Bonnie is a lovely name, but you should name her what you already had picked out."

Violet smiled down at her daughter. "Her name is Maeven Marie, and she is so beautiful.

Lester got up, came to Brody, and held out his hand. "I really appreciate what you did here tonight. We're beholding to you."

"All I ask is that you love your daughter and give her a good home. My reward was bringing a new life into this world," said Brody, who knew then that he would be a doctor someday.

Two sips of coffee was all the young man wanted. He

made a puckered face and gave the cup to Debbie and walked to Violet. "I'm a little embarrassed to ask this, but it's necessary. Has your milk come in yet?"

Grinning from ear to ear, she replied, "Oh yes, that's not an issue."

"Go ahead and see if Maeven will nurse," said Brody.

The baby latched on, and Brody excused himself to change his clothes.

With clean clothes on, he checked on Violet and Maeven again before retiring for the night. The events of the day caused him to think about what had transpired and how he took over with the childbirth. By helping Dr. Melrose so many times, he knew what to do. What an opportunity to help bring a new human into this world. Thoughts of his mother overtook his feelings. She would be so proud of him for helping Lester and Violet. His tired eyes became watery as he contemplated the stress his poor mother must be going through. She didn't know where he was or if her only son was still alive.

Brody wiped the tears from his eyes. Killing Ludwig had been necessary to save his and his mother's lives. Even though he was on the run, life would go on for his mother and for him.

The following morning, Brody woke up to see Bob, Lester, and Susan getting the fires going for coffee and breakfast. There was no talking or banging on pots and pans. He assumed they were letting the mother and her newborn sleep as long as possible. This was the prime time for the new doctor to begin his book learning. He shook out his boots, went to the wash pan, took two handfuls of water, and washed his face.

As he walked by everyone, he quietly said, "Good morning. I'm going to go study my medical books."

The Mosleys camped at the river for another four

days, fishing and hunting, while Violet recovered after giving birth. She was up doing light chores and taking short walks.

Brody spent each day hunting and studying medical books. The Moselys were friendly folks, and he appreciated their hospitality and what they taught him about traveling across the country. Their journey would soon cause them to turn south once they found the Chisholm Trail. The future had so many uncertain turns in it that Brody wasn't sure which direction to take when he left the small caravan.

Chapter Twelve

BRODY SAT WITH HIS BACK AGAINST A LARGE sycamore tree with the wagons between where he sat and the campfire. He had moved away from everyone so he could study without any interruptions. Thirty minutes later, a horse nickered on the other side of the wagons, but he didn't pay any attention to it until he heard loud, unfamiliar voices.

"Howdy folks, I'm Randolf Cody, and if you're planning on passing through here, then you have to pay me for your passage."

Brody laid his book down and moved closer to the wagon, where he could better hear the conversation with this Randolf person.

"Mister, this is Indian Territory, and I ain't never heard of anyone having to pay to cross over it," said Bob.

"I'm telling you here and now that you have to pay!" said Randolf, and then another voice called out, "Pa, you want Roy and me to see what's in these wagons?"

"No one is going to look in my wagons," said Bob in a shaky voice.

Brody could tell this was about to get out of hand and started biting his bottom lip before he pulled his pistol from its holster. With the hammer cocked back and the gun behind his back, he made his way to the last wagon and got in a position where he could see who was doing the talking.

All of the Mosleys except Violet were standing facing Randolf and his two boys. He could tell that Bob and Lester were both nervous by how sweaty their faces were. Randolf smiled and said, "Now look here. We intend on getting paid one way or another, so I reckon it's time the dickering is over, and you make me an offer."

Brody stepped from behind the wagon with the pistol pointed at Randolf.

"I do believe that I can kill you and at least one of your boys before the other one can get his gun out. Or I may be able to kill all three of you if he misses me."

Randolf sat with his hands on the saddle horn, surprised at the young man's sudden appearance, pointing a gun at him. "I know what you're thinking," said Brody. "Is he a good enough shot to get us all?" Brody took a step closer and continued, "And does he have the nerve to even try?"

Brody kept his eyes on Randolf. "Lester, my rifle is behind you against the wagon tongue."

Randolf pointed his index finger at Lester. "You stay put. I'll drop you if you go after that gun."

Brody smiled. "I'll kill the first one of you that moves! Lester, do as I say."

Lester backed to the wagon tongue and was reaching for the rifle when one of the younger men moved his hand to his gun butt. Brody fired, and with luck, it grazed the man's left shoulder, causing him to yelp out in pain and fall off his horse.

Brody had the pistol pointed back at Randolf. "Your boy is lucky that I'm a good shot, or he would be dead. I'm not playing with you men. He moved his hand to his gun, and it cost him. The next one will die. Now, load up your boy and get."

Lester had the rifle pointed at Randolf also, and the older man pointed to the son still on his horse. "Roy, get your brother loaded up, and let's get out of here." The man was getting off the ground, holding his shoulder. Roy helped his brother on his horse, and the three rode off.

Brody holstered his gun. "That was a close call. I think we should break camp and get away from here in case they come back looking for trouble."

Bob shook his head. "I don't think they'll come back."

Lester was still holding his rifle. "Pa, those men were going to rob us. If it hadn't been for Brody, no telling what they would have taken."

Susan walked over to Bob. "Brody's right. We need to skedaddle out of here and get as far away as possible. Bob, you, Lester, and Thomas get these wagons hooked up, and me and the girls will get our things secure."

Bob stood there staring at his wife until she touched his cheek with her hand. "We have to get going. Those men were going to rob us and no telling what else. So pull off your goody-two-shoes and get busy."

Lester and Thomas were already going after the livestock when Bob started after the yokes for the oxen. Brody knew nothing about gunfights or outlaws, but this incident made him realize that Bob couldn't be counted on in a fight.

With his horse saddled and all his gear loaded, Brody mounted up, carried his rifle in the crook of his arm, and rode off in the direction the Codys had left by. He was going to make sure that they didn't come back and attack his friends.

An hour later, Brody rode back to the abandoned campsite but could still see the wagons off in the distance. He rode south and stayed far enough back to watch the Mosley's backtrail.

Chapter Thirteen

THE MOSLEYS STOPPED A FEW MINUTES BEFORE dark. There was enough light to gather wood and buffalo chips for a couple of fires. Brody came into camp when he figured that supper was ready.

As they all sit in the firelight eating, Susan says, "Brody, we're grateful for what you did today. You're a brave young man to stand up for us, and I appreciate you."

"Mrs. Susan, you're my friends, and I wasn't going to stand by and let them steal you blind. I'm goin' to sleep about a hundred yards away just in case they want to come back in the dark."

"I can take my rifle and be on guard with you," said Lester.

Brody thought about that for a few seconds and said, "That's a good idea, but I want you over that way, and I'll be over this way. If they do come back, me and you can handle them."

NOTHING HAPPENED DURING THE NIGHT, and in the morning, the women cooked breakfast while the men hooked the oxen and horses to the wagons and gathered up the items that didn't involve their meal.

Brody stayed back a quarter of a mile to protect their backs and rode with the confidence that he was ready for any trouble. Being alone on the trail gave him time to think about what was next for him. He couldn't stay with the Mosleys much longer but couldn't leave them until he was confident they wouldn't have any more trouble. Bob and his good nature would get his family robbed or even killed, if he trusted everyone.

He thought back to Wichita and wondered how his poor mother was doing. He hoped she was more worried about him than she was missing that poor excuse of a man she had married. Ludwig should be rotting in the ground by now, and she should be in control of the bar. He only hoped she would step up and take over the management of the business.

The young man was interrupted by rumbling to the southwest of their location. He thought it could be thunder, but no clouds were overhead. Urging the horse to go faster for a half mile to the top of a hill, a dark storm cloud was forming in the southwest. This could be trouble if the storm was heading this way.

Brody urged his horse to go as fast as possible to catch up with the wagons. They could be in extreme danger if caught in the storm's path.

He slowed down when he was even with Bob in the lead wagon.

"Bob, we have to find cover. A huge storm is forming in the southwest, and we can't be caught in it."

"Go ahead and see if you can find us a gully where we can get the wagons out of harm's way of the storm.

We'll have to have a way out as soon as the leading side of the storm passes by, or we'll get bogged down," shouted Bob over the noise of the oxen hooves and wagons.

The boy was frantically looking for a ravine when he saw a hill where the east side of the mound was almost a sheer side. We could place the wagons beside the wall, protecting them from severe wind or a tornado.

He rode back in sight of the wagon, waited until they were close, and began to lead them where he found the hill. The thunder's rumbling was getting closer, and the wind was changing directions.

Bob positioned his wagon and then went back and brought the others in where the teams were up against the wagon in front of them.

Bob grabbed the ropes from under the wagon seat. "We need to hobble the lead oxen in case they get frightened and want to run off." Lester hopped down, and he and his pa put hobbles on all the animals while Brody rode up on top of the hill to observe the advancing storm.

The lightning could be seen dancing across the sky, and then it started to come out of the clouds in fingers toward the ground. The rumble was getting so intense that he could feel the ground shake. Brody wasn't sure what would happen, but he knew sitting on top of the hill wasn't safe. With only a nudge with his boot heels, the horse took off down the hill. A fierce finger of lightning descended from the black rotating cloud and struck a tree not two hundred yards south of the hill. Flames shot up the side of the tree trunk, and limbs shuddered and sailed away from the tree. Brody rode as fast as the horse would go, and when they arrived at the wagons, he tied his horse to one of the wheels. Lester came out of his wagon and helped Brody hobble the horse's front legs.

Bob had everyone take cover underneath the wagons when the wind increased, and the rain fell. With them so close to the cleft of the hill, only a little water was running under the wagons.

In a few minutes, the sky opened up, and torrential rain came down through the blowing wind. At times, the scared travelers thought the wagons were being lifted off the ground. The tempest was so intense that it sounded like a locomotive was going by them. The forceful wind and rain began to subside after fifteen minutes, and everyone's clothing was muddy and wet even though they were under the cover of the wagons.

Brody was the first one out and removed the hobbles off his horse so he could mount up. The rain was still coming down, but the wind had stopped. When he was back atop the hill, he could see a path of half a quarter where the ground was bare. That sound he heard was the all-encompassing noise of a tornado that had come way too close for comfort. He would remember this important lesson for future situations like this.

When he arrived back at the wagons, everyone was busy moving them where they could make camp and stake out the animals. One of the wagon covers had a large tear where a limb was still protruding through it.

"Don't you think we should remove that limb and keep going until nightfall?" asked Brody.

"Nope, we'll camp here tonight and give the soil time to soak up the rain. I'm afraid all we'll do is wear out the teams trying to pull through the mud today," said Bob, pointing to the cover. "We need to make repairs, or the hole will get bigger. I'd appreciate it if you and Thomas removed it so Susan can stitch it up.

"Sure thing, Bob," said Brody, and he dismounted, and in a few minutes, the two young men had the cover off.

Susan came over and put her hand on Brody's shoulder. "If we had some fresh meat, I could fry potatoes and bread with it. With this storm passing through, the wildlife may be on the move."

Brody picked up his rifle where he had put it against the wagon wheel. "That makes sense. I'll see if I can shoot some game for supper."

Susan put her hand on his shoulder. "Good, me and Violet will be getting everything else ready while you're gone."

Chapter Fourteen

NOT MORE THAN A MILE FROM CAMP, DUST could be seen on the horizon, and the closer he got to it, the sound of hooves filled his ears. With the rifle in hand, he topped a hill and discovered the largest herd of buffalo he had ever seen.

Growing up in Kansas, he had seen the massive beast occasionally, but this was much different. As far as he could see, they were spread out, running from the east to the west. He tried to take aim, but it would be an impossible shot for this distance to hit a running target.

Brody kicked his horse's ribs and took off toward the herd, and as he got closer, he rode close to a young bull and fired twice, before its front legs buckled and it toppled over. The sound of gunfire caused the herd to run faster, and the young hunter turned his horse to stay out of their path.

Five minutes later, the herd passed by, and it was time to butcher the young buffalo. He had to think a few seconds where to start and decided to try and skin it like Lester had shown him on the deer. The skinning process wasn't going that well with the beast lying on the ground. He reevaluated what to do and decided to remove the hind quarters and shoulder that the animal wasn't lying on.

He then rolled the carcass over and removed the other hind quarter. That was all he could carry back on his horse, and it was most likely more than they could eat.

He hated that the rest of the meat was left behind, but the coyotes and buzzards had to eat, too.

Bob and Lester helped skin the hide off the portions he brought back. Lester motioned with his fingers. "The next time, start on the leg and work your way up onto the hind quarter. That way, you can pull the hide back and get to the meat before you remove it from the animal."

———

AFTER SUPPER, Brody went to his horse and headed out a hundred yards from the Mosley's camp. He wanted to read some more in the medical books, but that would require a fire, and that would give away his location if they had visitors.

The young man was getting homesick and kept thinking about how his mother was doing. Maybe if he came to a town, he could send her a telegram or a letter. This was Indian Territory, and he didn't even know if there were towns here, let alone a telegraph office or a post office.

———

THE FOLLOWING MORNING, Brody and the Mosleys left out with cloudy, overcast skies. Bob said, "We need to push the teams today in case it decides to rain." Three hours later, they rode up to the Chisholm Trail, where another group of eleven wagons were heading south along the east edge of the pathway.

Brody rode up to the lead wagon and said to Bob and Susan, "This is where I leave you folks. I'm heading southeast from here in hopes of finding a doctor that I can work for. It's been my pleasure riding with you all."

Bob leaned over and stuck out his hand. "Thank you, young man. We appreciate all you've done and especially for helping Violet and Lester."

After saying goodbye to the rest of the Mosleys, he rode southwest in hopes of making his own path through unknown territory.

The sun was beginning to make its way toward the west when he rode upon five sod houses built in a semi-circle and a large corral with two holding pens that took up the space in the opening. A water well was in the middle of the yards, and he figured whoever lived here had hand-dug the well. Five yelping, cur dogs came from three of the houses, barking and running toward Brody and his horse.

An Indian man came out from a lean-to shed that was in one of the holding pens and hollered at the dogs. In the livestock pen, the boy could see horses and mules grazing inside the wooden pole corral.

Brody was a little apprehensive about riding on in but was in need of water for his horse and himself. The water well had a bucket hanging by a rope over a pulley, and a hollowed-out log served as a water trough.

"Hello, I'm needing water for my horse and my

canteen. May I draw a bucket from your well?" he asked the man by the shed.

The man waved his hand into the air and said, "Go away."

Brody was a little taken aback by the man. "Sir, all I want is water for me and my horse."

"White man bring sickness and we die," said the Indian and reached down and picked up a bow. Brody pulled his gun from its holster and said, "I ain't sick and I'm not going to give anyone anything. But I'll go and leave you be."

He was about to argue with the man some more until he heard coughing from inside the house nearest him. It was a deep cough, and whoever was sick had lots of congestion.

"I'll be leaving now," said the boy, and turned his horse toward the south. He didn't know what those folks had, but it wasn't something he wanted to be exposed to out here without any modern medicine.

Two miles south, he came up to a creek and let his horse drink his fill. Brody still hadn't been in the wild long enough to trust drinking creek water, so he built a small fire and boiled his water. All his provisions were gone except for a tin of beans, and he went ahead and ate those while he was waiting on his drinking water.

While letting the water cool, he stood with his arms to his side and started to practice drawing the pistol. It was awkward at first, but the more he practiced, the smoother it got. He didn't fire the weapon, because he didn't want to waste his ammunition. This went on for almost an hour and then he filled his canteen and drank down what was left of the purified water.

With a change in directions to follow the creek since he had heard that most settlements were by bodies of water, if he was lucky, maybe he could shoot a deer or turkey for supper. Not far from where he had watered his horse, a rabbit ran out of the brush and stopped a short distance away. Brody removed the rifle and was taking aim when the furry critter decided to hop off. Brody whistled, and the rabbit stopped for the last time. It only took one shot, and the boy had his supper.

He went ahead and gutted the hare before he continued on to find a good place to camp.

Chapter Fifteen

A CAMPSITE WAS CHOSEN WHERE THE CREEK turned, and the grass along the bank was plentiful for the young explorer's horse. Clouds were forming in the west, and there seemed to be a smell of rain in the air. He didn't have anything to protect himself from the rain, and the next time he was at a store, a rain slicker would be his next purchase. Then he thought about the ground tarp he had with his bedroll.

He didn't want to get wet and sick, so he made a small lean-to between two trees and used the ground tarp to keep the rain off. The ground would be damp, so he cut smaller trees, trimmed the limbs, and laid them on the ground so he wouldn't get wet.

Next, he built a fire close by and cooked the rabbit. By the time the fire was blazing and a few coals were formed, he had the small animal skinned and ready to cook.

The rain stayed away long enough for the wannabe doctor to read one of the medical books by the light from the fire. He was getting sleepy when the rain began to lightly come-down. The ground tarp kept the rain off, and he snuggled up against his saddle, covered with his bedding, and went to sleep.

Thunder woke the young man up sometime before daylight. He stayed under his covering and saw the lightning dance across the skies. There was enough light from the striking energy for him to see his horse not more than twenty feet away. The animal seemed unfazed and continued to graze even with the loud noise.

Not being able to go back to sleep, Brody thought about how well he drew his gun yesterday. He would practice every day, and he may become fast like one of the western gunfighters he had heard of. He had read about John Wesley Harden and Will Bill and listened to his dead stepfather talk about Clay Allison. Ludwig had said that Clay was the fastest gunfighter ever.

Thinking about Ludwig, it was rumored in Wichita that Ludwig and his cronies had killed men who crossed them at the bar. The law had come to their house one time and took the mean bar owner to jail, but they had to turn him loose the next day.

Ludwig had always sold rum at his bar and said he knew rum runners that brought the stout liquor in from Canada. He knew many people across the country and had even worked as a longshoreman in his younger days.

Brody still didn't have any quims about killing the man who had beaten him for years. His mother had put up with the man way too long, and she deserved much better. Taking the life of another human was not something he ever thought he would do, but there comes a time when a man has to stand on his own two feet and do what has to be done. That's what he did. He took it up on his shoulders and actually did it without getting shot himself.

Dr. Melrose seemed to know what would happen the last time he and the doctor talked. He advised an escape route and figured the doctor knew what would happen.

Sunlight was nonexistent through the early morning sky and cast a dreary feeling over the day when Brody finally got out from under his shelter and wiped the water off his horse with a handful of grass. The rain hadn't stopped, but it was down to a drizzle when he took off, crossed the creek, and headed south.

He had bought a coat in Oxford, and with that on, he would stay dry for a while. The slow, soaking rain with no sun or wind had made the ground muddy and slick. The streams and gullies had water running through them, and he kept looking for a place to hold up and wait out the rain.

A strange-looking formation was off to his right. It looked like double hills, and there might be someplace between the hills where he could get out of the weather.

Riding between the hills was more than he imagined. It turned out to be a backside, and instead of two hills, it was one huge hill in the shape of a horseshoe. He kept riding, and after half a mile, the opening between the sides opened up into a vast meadow where horses and cows grazed.

Walking the horse through the herd, he saw a sod and wood house built at the back of the property. Pulling the rifle from its scabbard, he continued on toward the house. Two dogs began to bark and came toward him. A man came out carrying a rifle and took aim.

The man was short and stocky, bowlegged with long gray hair. He had on Indian made buckskins and a vest made out of hides. Brody didn't know what to do, so he rode toward the house. When he was in talking distance, he said, "Hello, I mean you no harm. I come in peace."

The man raised the rifle to his shoulder. "You have sick?"

Brody shook his head. "No sir, I'm healthy." He continued on to within thirty feet of the man. "As you can see, I'm not sick. What kind of sickness are you talking about?"

"Cholera, and the family dies. White gives sick to Indians," said the old man.

"Did your family die of the disease?"

The Indian pointed to the west where the remains of a fire had been. "We build a fire and burn the dead."

"I'm Brody Connor, and I'm studying to be a doctor. I don't know if I can help, but I'm willing to help if I can."

"I am William Longtooth, and all my family has died. No one here but me. I am the healer of my tribe, but my medicine no good for cholera."

"Maybe I can learn from you how you heal people. I've heard that Indian medicine men have plants they use for different conditions. I can use what you teach me to help people."

William was shaking his head. "No! I use the spirits along with plants to heal. White men can't call on the spirits. You go now."

Brody looked around and saw a barn behind the house. "Can I stay in your barn until the rain stops? I promise you I won't cause you any problems."

The man stared at Brody and then said, "You use the barn, but stay away from the house." William turned and went back into the dwelling.

Brody rode to the barn, unsaddled his horse, took his things inside, and made himself comfortable. He was hungry but didn't have anything to eat, so he took his rifle and went outside, hoping to go hunting for game to eat. As he started across the field with his rifle, William came to the back door and called, "Where you go?"

Brody turned toward him. "I'm hungry and going to find food."

William motioned with his arm. "Come back, I have food."

Brody followed him inside the house, where he had meat and potatoes on the table. The two ate together in silence, and when they were finished, the old man got up and filled two cups with a dark liquid that Brody thought was coffee, but it wasn't. "What is this? It's really good.

"Boiled roots of the sassafras tree."

Brody smacked his lips together. "It's delicious. I'll find a school where I can study and learn to be a real doctor."

"You can move your things into the house. If the Great Spirit comes for me, you can be comfortable at least."

"Thanks, William. I'll go get my belongings."

Chapter Sixteen

THE BOY STAYED WITH THE OLD MAN, WHOM HE referred to as the *Healer*, for the first two days. Brody was taught about plants that had healing powers for different ailments. The Healer made the boy small leather bags so he could put the different seeds, ground-up leaves, and ground roots in to keep them separated.

Brody was in hog heaven, learning about plants and how to make a poultice to eliminate infections. The Healer showed him how to call on the Great Spirit in times of sickness and injuries. All this was new to the boy, and he had a hard time comprehending it all.

On the third day with the old man, two young Indian girls came to the house speaking in their native language. Still, Brody knew that something was wrong by the excitement and urgency in their voices.

When they had spoken to the old medicine man, he said, "Saddle your horse and bring all your belongings. We go see their sick mama."

Brody saddled up his horse and stowed his books and

clothes on his horse while the old man saddled his mule. One of the girls rode with Brody, and one with William.

They had to travel close to five miles until they arrived at a large sod house. Brody had dismounted when William said, "You care for animals and then come in."

"Yes, sir."

Chanting and the rattling of gourds could be heard outside before Brody entered the house. The woman was lying on hides and blankets in the middle of the floor, and the Healer was chanting and moving his hands, with his fingers spread out over her body from head to feet.

The two girls, two men, an old woman, and three more children were in a circle around the woman. They were chanting and shaking their gourds, crying out to the Great Spirit.

Brody knelt beside the woman and looked at William. "What do you think it is?"

The Healer pointed to her abdomen. "Her side and belly are angry. It hurts bad."

Brody kneeled beside her. "Has she been puking?"

William spoke to the woman whose face was covered in sweat. She nodded her head and said something to William.

"She said that it started yesterday and that she can't eat or drink anything."

"I need to see and feel her stomach. Will that be all right?" asked Brody.

William spoke to the woman and the others before he said, "You touch."

Brody began to undo her dress but stopped and placed a blanket over her breast before he opened up the dress. He began to press on her belly and right side until she almost came up off the bedding. She cried out in pain and could hardly breathe.

Brody looked at William. "We have to operate, and it may save her life. Either her appendix or gallbladder has ruptured, and she will die if we don't go in and remove it."

William nodded his head as if he understood and started talking to the others. After some exchange of words with the others, he turned back to Brody. "You do it. I help. I have never cut anyone open for healing. What you need?"

Brody looked around the room and pointed to the kitchen table. "I need to use the table, but first, we need scalding water to clean it. I'll need sharp knives of different sizes and boiled hair from the horse's tail. I'll need a couple of sewing needles and rags. We must boil all the knives, hair, needles, and rags."

William spoke to the others in the room, and they started gathering what Brody would need.

Brody pointed to William's medicine pouches. "Do you have anything that will make her go to sleep?"

William began to remove the pouches from around his neck and waist belt. "I grind Jimson weeds into powder and mix it like a tea from the Black Willow. I can make a paste of the Jimson for the wound."

Brody was looking at the light in the room. "That will have to work. Go ahead and get it started."

William spoke to the man, who got up and went outside.

"All right, let's get busy," said Brody. "We'll need a lot more light in here for me to see."

The man came back in carrying a half-gallon fruit jar full of moonshine. He handed it to William, who said, "We back up the tea with this."

"We'll also use it to disinfect all our instruments. I need to see where the cooking utensils are, and we'll need to keep the fire going so I can cauterize the places inside her to stop the bleeding."

William pointed to the whiskey jar. "There's more of the whiskey."

"Good. We need to keep the wound sanitary so she doesn't get an infection. After the instruments are boiled, place them in a pan of whiskey. I'm going to get whatever I can find to help. You and I will have to scrub our hands before we begin the surgery."

The next hour was spent where everyone was working together, getting everything ready for Brody and William to get started.

William began to give the woman sips of the tea that was also mixed with the alcohol. She had a hard time drinking the stuff but was able to keep it down long enough for it to start to work.

Chapter Seventeen

Brody took William to the wash bowl and had him scrub his hands and arms with lye soap. "While I'm cutting the woman open, I'll need you to help hold her down. She's going to feel most of this, but hopefully, she'll pass out, and it will give me the time I need to perform the surgery."

"Do you need any others to help?" asked William.

"Yes, I'll need someone to help you hold her down, and I'll need both of the older girls to help. One will blot off the blood, and the other one will keep us clean rags to use. This will be bloody, but I can't help that."

"You tell me what you need, and I'll speak to the others," said William.

With everyone in place and four lanterns hanging from the rafters, Brody washed off the woman's stomach with moonshine and made the cut where he had seen Dr. Melrose do the same surgery in the past. Although he had never used the knife, he had blotted up the blood and watched with intensity to know he would do it someday.

As he made the incision along the lower right quadrant of the abdomen, the woman screamed out and went stiff. She then jerked and passed out. That gave the young man time to finish the cut and pry the incision open where he could see what was ailing the poor woman. He had one of the girls blot the blood away long enough to move things around enough to see the appendix inflamed, infected, and swollen. He worked carefully, locating where to make the cut to remove the organ and had one of the girls take a knife to the fire and get the tip of the blade red hot. When he finally removed the little organ, he applied the tip of the knife and seared off the blood. He then poured a small portion of the alcohol into the wound and blotted as much of it as he could.

"William, tell the girl to bring me the needle and hair. All we have to do is sew her up and hope she comes awake later. While I'm stitching her up would be a good time to call on the Great Spirit to watch over her."

Everyone in the house chanted and shook the gourds the entire time it took to stitch up the wound and clean it with the moonshine. When Brody was finally finished, he went to the wash basin and washed his hands and arms off.

"William, I would appreciate it if you would make a poultice to go on the wound. We need to keep the infection and pain down if we can. I would also like to move her to a bed and get her off the table so the girls can clean it."

Brody went to one of the chairs and sat down to rest from being physically and mentally drained. He had worked on the woman for almost two hours, and he knew he had to wait to see if she ever woke up again.

The girls cooked supper while the father cared for the

animals. Brody moved his chair so he could keep a wet rag on the woman's forehead and feel her face for fever. Dr. Melrose was a stickler for keeping everything sterile to minimize infection and with what was available here, the young man wasn't sure how good his preparation worked.

After supper, when everyone was getting ready to go to sleep, the woman moaned in her state of unconsciousness. Brody began to wipe her face with the cool rag, and in another hour, she opened her eyes.

The sick woman tried to talk, but Brody put a finger on her lip. "I'll get you some water." Not knowing if she understood, he woke William up to translate. "The patient is awake. Go see what she says while I get her a drink of water."

With a dipper of water in his hand, and with the help of William, they raised her enough where she could drink. William smiled when the woman began to talk. "She said she saw the Great Spirit on the other side, and he sent her back down here. You did good, Brody Connor."

Brody nodded his head up and down, smiling at what he heard. "If the Great Spirit sent her back, I reckon the surgery worked. I'm going to make my bed on the floor to be close to her tonight. You go back to sleep, and if I need you, I'll come get you."

The following morning, Brody woke before daylight to the woman's moans. He felt her forehead to find that she was a little warm and began to put wet towels on her exposed skin. By the time everyone was coming awake, she was snoring, and that pleased the young doctor.

On the second day after the surgery, the woman was helped up and walked inside the house for a few minutes before she sat down and had a bowl of soup.

That night, William handed Brody the jar of moonshine. "Tomorrow I go home. You stay."

Brody handed the stout liquor back. "I don't drink whiskey, and I don't want to go away until I remove the stitches and make sure she is going to be well."

After the first two nights, Brody moved his bed to a better location and remained awake, reminiscing about the surgery. The boy was proud that he had paid attention to Dr. Melrose and studied the medical books he had stolen. Just the mere thought of what he had done since he left Wichita brought a smile to his face. He had removed the bullet from the man he shot and delivered a baby into this world to a lovely family. Now, he had actually performed surgery and most likely saved a woman's life.

None of these accomplishments could have been performed if he hadn't worked for the doctor and learned from him. He was learning that life had a way of putting him in a position where he could help, which was a good thing.

The woman continually had a fever for the next two days but was then able to resume many of her daily duties. After a full week, the incision looked so good that he gave it two more days and then removed the stitches.

Brody had become bored after reading through all his medical books and would saddle his horse and go hunting. He was able to bring back a deer on his second day out.

The weather turned violent, with thunder, lightning, wind, and rain. He couldn't go out, so he stayed in and started reading one of the books for a second time.

On the ninth day, he removed the horsehair stitches and put a poultice on the incision made from the herbs and plants that William had left him. The language barrier was his biggest problem, but he learned what some words were when the family talked to him by pointing and saying the word.

He would stay one more night and let the storm pass before he left. Not sure where he would go, the young man lay on his bed that night and thought about his future and where he should go when he left. Would he go back to William's and learn more about the natives' healing, or would he wander somewhere else? He still wanted to go to doctor school, but unless there was a school south, he may have to put that on hold.

Brody began to think of home and his mother. How was she coping with him being gone and on the run? Was the law out looking for him? Were there wanted posters with his face on them and a reward for his capture?

Chapter Eighteen

THE FOLLOWING MORNING, THE PATIENT WAS still doing good and recovering nicely when Brody checked on her. He ate breakfast with the family and packed up his possessions. With his horse saddled and waiting out front, the young man went back inside and said, "I'm leaving now, and it's been my pleasure staying here." He knew they most likely didn't understand him, so he hugged the females and shook hands with the males.

The husband of the woman he operated on handed the young doctor a rolled-up hide and said, "Wado, unali, donadagohvi."

Brody unrolled the hide, which was a vest made out of deer skin. He put it on and said, "Donadagohvi unali." He had learned the words meant *until we meet again, friend*.

Brody mounted up and turned north in the direction of William's house. The old man had helped him tremendously, and it would be wrong to leave without telling him thanks. The rain the day before had left the ground soft, and the streams were running deeper with the fresh water.

Not two miles from the old man's house, Brody saw a spike buck, and with one shot, the small deer went down. This kill would provide his friend with meat for a few days. All he did was gut the deer and cut off the head so it would be easier to haul on the back of his horse.

William was waiting under the tree that he used to skin animals when Brody came to a stop and dismounted. "Hello, William. I brought meat for your belly."

William smiled and held up his skinning knife. "Bring him here and I skin him."

Brody held the small buck up while William tied the back hooves with rope and proceeded to skin the deer. Brody knew better than to try and talk to the old guy while he worked, so he sat down and watched the pro at work.

William cut the meat into chunks where it could be carried inside, and he looked at Brody. "Take meat, we go inside."

Brody carried a load inside and then went back out for the rest of it while William drew a bucket of water to wash his hands and arms. With the meat on the table, the old man stoked up the fire and put lard in a skillet and filled it with sliced meat.

When it was cooking, William turned to Brody and made a circle with his hand. "Four moons ago, two men came looking for you. Bad men, say you kill. I told them you went to the North Canadian River Settlement."

Brody almost fainted in front of his friend, but instead he gathered the strength and said, "I did kill a man. He beat me and my ma. I was scared that he would kill her, and I shot him."

The old Indian didn't change his expression, but he did put down the knife and looked into the frightened young man's eyes. "I kill many red and white men in my youth. I went to White man school and ran off to join the great chief Red Cloud. I am healer and not killer, so I left Red Cloud and came here. Those men that came here will kill you for money. I can teach you how to fight, but you have to have the spirit of death in you to survive."

Brody sat there listening to the wise old man talk. It was a lot to take in, and he needed to know more about what William was going to teach him. "I would like for you to teach me how to survive. What do I need to learn?"

William stuck the knife blade into the tabletop. "We eat and then I teach you how to fight with a knife."

After the two men finished cooking up most of the meat and storing it in clay pots, William took Brody outside. There he set up targets and showed the young man how to hold the knife by the blade and how to throw it at the target. Brody spent the rest of the afternoon throwing the knife and recovering it from the dirt. It took him over an hour to hit the target for the first time. In another hour, he was hitting it seven out of ten throws.

"Stop and rest," said William, and brought over the water bucket and a gourd made into a dipper. "You have the feel now, and it's time to broaden your training." The old man wrapped hides on his hands and arms. "Come at me with the knife."

Brody held the knife the way he was shown earlier and came at William, striking at his hands. William swung his arm knocking the hand with the knife in it out of the way. The Indian then took the knife and showed Brody how to slash and jab with the blade. "You not only use knife but feet and other hand. You kick and hit and when there is opening, you stab and cut.

"I show you how native use knife now." The old warrior held the handle in his hand with the blade pointing at Brody. The old Indian began to circle the boy, weaving the knife blade as he moved. Suddenly, William went down on his right knee and swept Brody's legs out from under him with his extended left leg. As Brody fell to the ground, William lunged on him and was in the position to strike him with the knife.

The boy had a frightened expression on his face and knew at that moment that he had to pay attention and learn from the older man. "Will you show me how you did that so I can learn how to fight in close quarters?"

The rest of the afternoon was spent with the old man showing the young fighter different moves and ways to be the aggressor in battle. Both men were tired at the end of the day and sat outside to watch the sunset.

William pointed out across the land. "You learn to watch your surroundings and plan your attack. Never fight on their terms and always have an escape route. Tomorrow we fight with gun and horse." The old man raised up on tired legs and went inside to sleep.

Brody sat outside a while longer, thinking about what he had learned today and the fact that if he survived in this rugged place, those skills could save his life. Learning to fight with a gun would be fun tomorrow, and hopefully the old man would give him pointers on how to improve the speed of his draw.

Killing Ludwig hadn't taken any drawing skills or even sharpshooting ability. He had walked in, pointed the gun, tripped on a chair leg, and pulled the trigger. Yes, it could be considered murder, but in his mind, it was an accident and self-perseverance for him and his mother. Ludwig would have eventually hurt his mother so severely that it would kill her, and Brody wasn't going to let that happen.

When there was a way to send his ma a letter, he would do that to see how she was doing. Then he thought about the two men looking for him. William had said they were wanting money to kill him. There must be a reward out on him for dead or alive? Surely, killing a tavern owner didn't warrant that kind of reward. Ludwig had a lot of enemies, and the law was always watching him.

Those were the reflections that flooded the young man's thoughts until he went inside and lay on his bedroll.

During the night, rain began to fall, and the temperature fell where it woke Brody up enough to get out of bed and put wood on the fire. He sat in front of the blazing wood, thinking about the men hunting him and was startled when William put a hand on his shoulder. "Never stare into the flames. When you look away, you can't see,"

Brody turned his eyes away from the flames and sure enough his vision wasn't clear. Another lesson he had to hone on his journey of survival.

"Go back to bed, long day ahead in the rain," said William, and went back to his bed. Brody followed his advice and lay back down.

Chapter Nineteen

THE FOLLOWING MORNING, THE RAIN WAS STILL falling, and the temperature outside had dropped considerably since yesterday. William stood in the doorway looking out across the land. "Come," said the older man, motioning to Brody, who walked and stood beside his mentor.

Brody looked out at the rain. "What do you want me to do?"

Again, William waved his arm across the land before them. "Look out there and tell me what you see." The old warrior went to his chair to sit.

Brody had no clue what he was supposed to be looking at as he swept the land from right to left. "I don't see anything."

"You not looking. Take time, look closer." Again, William swept his arm across the land. "Lots to see."

Brody again began to search with his eyes and then it dawned on him what was out there. Birds would fly over the land. An armadillo scurried around looking for grubs. Further out was a coyote hunting for his next meal.

Brody began to tell William what he saw, and the older man came to stand beside him.

"You see with your eyes, but you also see with your ears. Listen to the sounds. You hear rain, but there are other noises that you don't listen for. The birds, the animals walking across leaves. The change in sounds means something. You have to listen and see."

Brody did what the old man said, and soon he could make out different sounds other than the rain hitting the ground or falling on the grass roof of the house. As he recognized a different sound, he would describe it to his friend.

The rain slackened off, and William took the boy outside and tied a handkerchief around his head where he couldn't see. Holding Brody by the arm, the Indian led the way to the livestock shed and went inside. He removed the blindfold. "Go find the pitchfork."

Brody took two steps and tripped over a shovel lying on the ground. He raised himself up from the ground and said, "I didn't see that shovel on the ground."

"When you go inside, wait until you can see before walking," said William. "Your eyes can see in the dark if you give them time to adjust. Now saddle your horse."

With Brody in the saddle, William showed him how to maneuver his body so he could get low in the saddle to avoid getting shot. The young man was shown how to hang onto the side of the horse and fire his gun underneath the neck of his mount in a running battle. By noon it was time to practice what he had learned that morning. William had targets on trees, and Brody would come riding by and get himself in position and fire under the horse's neck as he passed the targets. After much practice shots, the bullets began to hit the targets.

By late afternoon, Brody was feeling more confident

in his abilities until William said, "It's time to start with your draw. You have holster too low and need to fix that."

Brody put his hand on the gun butt. "I thought it would be faster to draw if I wore it low."

"If too low, you have to bring arm up to aim. Try it up a little," said William, as he moved the holster up and had Brody draw time after time to show him that it was more in the wrist action and not the shoulder or elbow. After many minutes of drawing, it was time to practice hitting a target.

William went through the motions. "Start slow, pull gun, point and shoot."

Brody drew, brought the gun up to eye level and shot, missing the target.

William pushed his arm down. "No! Use finger as gun. Draw, point finger and shoot."

Brody again started, and William hit his arm. "No, not that way. Like this." The old man pulled the gun from the holster, pointed, and fired from the hip.

Brody began to do it the way he was directed, and the bullets began to hit their mark. Practice went on until he was almost out of ammunition, and then William had him stop.

"We stop and cook. Tomorrow we go to trading post for more ammunition."

After supper, Brody had tried to remember all the things he had been taught over the last few days. He was deep in thought when William came and sat across from him with more pointers. "Always fight with the sun to your back. Never fight close to high noon. With the sun to your back, you have the advantage even with a stronger opponent. You pick the time and place, and if you can take the opponent by surprise, then the advantage is yours."

"That's well and good, but what if someone picks a fight with me. What do I do?"

"You strike first always. Never give the other man time to defend himself," said William. "A man can be nice and let the other man hit him first, but the chance of him winning is slim. You always hit first, you shoot first."

"How far is the trading post from here?" asked Brody.

"Half day away. Not far."

"Could those two men who's looking for me, be there tomorrow?"

"Maybe, or maybe not. We find out tomorrow. Go to bed."

Brody lay on his bedroll and thought about becoming a fighter and how much he appreciated William for all his hard work. If the two bounty hunters were at the trading post, he would have to cross that stream when he got to it. There was no need pondering on it tonight. With that said, the young man went to sleep.

Chapter Twenty

THE FOLLOWING MORNING, WILLIAM HAD EGGS cooking when Brody woke up and went outside. Most meals eaten at William's house were consumed in silence, and today was no different. Brody figured that talking while eating was something that Indians didn't do. The same thing had happened while he was staying with the family of the woman he did surgery on.

The two men headed out with Brody riding his horse and William on his mule, who only had one speed and that was slow. No wonder it was a half-day trip to the trading post. William seemed pleased with the animals' speed and every-so-often, Brody would have to wait on them.

The buildings at the store location were coming into view before William said, "One man rode a red horse and the other a black horse. The man on red horse was in charge. If they here, shoot first."

"I can see horses tied in front of the bigger building, but I don't see a black one," said Brody. "What are the other buildings?"

"Two Indian houses and two white houses," said William.

"Are they friendly?"

"I reckon so," said William, and adjusted the barrel of his rifle to the crook of his arm. "Have gun ready now, and hold reins in other hand."

Brody removed the safety strap off his pistol and swapped the reins to his left hand. It took the young man a few seconds to understand why he needed his right hand free to draw the pistol.

William directed his mule over to a small corral that housed two horses. Brody started to the hitch rail where the other horses were tied, but when William coughed, the boy came over and tied his mount beside the mule.

"If trouble, don't want men stealing horse to escape," said William, and walked toward the door. Inside the dark building, William waited until his eyes adjusted to the darkness. Brody stood beside him and understood the lessons he had been taught. A sweep of the room revealed a lantern over the counter cluttered with stacks of material, hides, and jars of hard candy.

To the left of the counter was two tables and four chairs, and sitting at the table were three men drinking from half-gallon buckets, that Brody assumed was beer. The far wall had shelves from about chest high to the rafters. Under the shelves were tables covered in cooking utensils, more material, clothes, and boots.

Brody's gaze went back to the three men, who had on hats, handkerchiefs, long-sleeve shirts and vests made from material. Each man was armed with pistols, and the boy could see that two of the men wore large rowel spurs. These men were likely cowboys from a ranch close by or off a trail drive and heading home.

The owner of the place came through the back door

with another bucket of beer and said, "Morning, William, I'll be with you directly as soon as I top off these fellers' beer."

William just nodded his head and waited on the man. When the feller walked behind the counter, he asked, "What do you need today?"

William pointed to Brody. "Friend needs ammunition."

Brody stepped forward. "I would like .41 caliber Colt ammunition, sir."

The man turned to the shelves behind him. "How many boxes do you want?"

Brody moved where he could see how many there was. "I'll take them all."

The man counted with his fingers. "I have eight boxes and they're two dollars a box."

Brody pulled his money from his pocket. "I want them all." He then turned to William. "Do we need anything at the house for food?"

William nodded his head. "Bacon, flour, salt, meal, and hard candy."

The man looked at Brody. "Get what he wants, and I'll pay."

One of the men sitting at the table spoke up. "Since you're so generous with that Indian, how about paying for our beer?"

Brody started biting his bottom lip before he pulled his gun from the holster. He held the gun behind his back, before he moved away from the counter and squared his hips toward the men. "Not today, fellers."

The man pushed his chair back a half foot and that's when Brody brought the gun around and pointed it at the cowboy. "Mister, I said not today and that's what I mean. If you get up, it'll be the last thing you ever do."

Brody had taken the man by surprise with his aggressive nature, and the other two were in no position to get in on the action. The man slowly placed his hands on the arms of the chair and slid it forward.

"I don't like trouble, so I'm thinking it would be to your advantage to place both your hands on top of the table and have a few more swallows of beer," said Brody, whose heart was beating so strong he thought the men could see it pulsating through his shirt.

The man who had been doing the talking said, "Mister, you're on the verge of making us mad, and that's not going to go over well for you."

Brody cocked back the hammer on his gun. "I'm sorry if I'm causing you to be uncomfortable, but if it comes down to you or me dying, then you win the prize. Me and my friend are going to get our provisions and walk out of here and never see you again."

The store owner put the items in a flour sack and placed it on the counter. "That will be another two dollars."

Brody pulled his money and handed it to the man. "Take out two dollars and give me the rest." William took the sack and went outside while Brody stayed with the men he had covered with his gun. He gave the old Indian time to get away before he backed to the door and took off running to his horse that had been moved closer to the door.

Brody was running his horse to catch up with William when he looked back to see the three men standing outside the trading post watching him. William had the mule running to put distance between them and the men when Brody caught up with him.

Brody looked at his mentor. "That was an interesting morning."

"You didn't shoot them."

"I didn't think it was necessary. They were just cowboys heading home."

William smiled. "You did good, for someone that was scared."

"I was scared. Did it show that much?"

"No, but I know things, I'm a healer," said William, smiling at his student.

"The good thing is, I have lots of ammunition to use."

William stopped his mule and pointed back the way they had come. "Men gone now. Go back and buy another gun. I saw a Colt and that is better gun."

Brody looked at the old man with confusion. "You want me to go back there and buy a gun?"

The old man nodded his head up and down. "Go back and buy a gun. Sam will know the one."

Brody turned back toward the trading post and started off muttering to himself about having to buy another gun.

The men were gone, and the store owner fixed the young man up with a Colt .45 caliber, and ten boxes of shells.

Chapter Twenty-One

THE FOLLOWING WEEKS WAS MORE TRAINING ON fighting techniques and instruction on how to stay alive. William used his leather-working skills to rework the holster to accommodate the new Colt so the young man could draw it smoother and faster. The .41 caliber pistol became Brody's backup gun, and William made him a holster where the pistol could be carried under the boy's left arm out of sight.

Each day, William took the time to show the young healer the different plants used for their healing powers. Ground-up leaves were used from some plants, and the roots boiled in water for other ailments.

By the end of the second month, Brody was once again getting low on ammunition from all the target practice.

While eating supper that night, Brody said, "William, I'm getting low on ammunition and I think it's time I move on south. I don't want those men to come back here looking for me and take the chance of you getting hurt. I'm thinking about riding south and see if I can find a post office or a telegraph office so I can let my ma know that I'm okay."

The old man didn't say anything or make any jesters until he had time to ponder on what the boy told him. After a few minutes, the healer pushed his bowl away. "You a man now and know what the Great Spirit has for you. Tomorrow you go south and the Great Spirit will go with you, my friend."

Brody didn't sleep well that night knowing he would be leaving the next morning to unknown places. He didn't know where he was going, but knew he had to leave here and make his own way. Although the future was uncertain, the one thing he did have was the ability to defend himself and the knowledge of the Indian way of healing others.

That following morning, Brody saddled his horse and loaded his gear before William approached the young man and gave him an embracing hug. "Brody Connor, you, my friend, are welcome in my lodge anytime. Keep helping people and remember what I taught you in a fight." The old man turned Brody loose and walked back inside his house.

Brody rode off with sadness in his heart, but it was time to leave and pursue his destiny. The two bounty hunters were out here somewhere, but that wasn't as much concern today as it had been over a week ago. William had taught him well, and the young man knew that he could fight with the best of them.

A mile south of William's house, the lone rider turned west in hopes of finding a trading post close to the Chisholm Trail. The other reason was simple. If the bounty hunters came back to William's, the old man wouldn't know where he went.

An hour after high noon, Brody came to the

Chisholm Trail, and on the far side was a small settlement. By the look of the surrounding landscape, farming and raising cattle was the main source of income. There were multiple plowed fields, and the closer he came to town, the more prominent his suspicions were by the businesses along the single business street. At the edge of town was a seed cleaning warehouse, and next to it was a freight company, a farm equipment yard, and farther on was a hardware store, café, and a saloon.

Brody saw a sign that had *Hennessey's Place* painted on it. Not wanting to spend much time here, the young man stopped at the only store and went inside where a lady came to him and asked, "Is there something I can get for you?"

"Yes, ma'am. I need bacon, flour, salt and two cans of beans if you have any."

She started writing his items down on a small slip of paper. "How much do you want of each?"

Brody was stumped. "I don't rightly know. I'll have to carry it on my horse, so maybe two days' worth."

"I'll fix you up," said the lady. "By the way, I have freshly baked biscuits and ham if you're interested."

"That sounds good. I also need two boxes of .41 and .45 shells if you have them."

While the woman gathered up his provisions, Brody wandered around the store and found a slicker and a new wide-brim hat. The slicker was needed, and the hat looked more cowboy than the one the city slicker currently wore.

It took a little work, but he finally had everything that was purchased secured on the horse. It was still a few hours until darkness when he thought about what to do, he really didn't want to make camp so early in the day, but he didn't want to spend the night here either. What he needed more than anything was information about what was to the south of the little settlement. The sound of a hammer hitting metal caused the young man to look south down the dusty street and see a wagon parked in front of a shed. The right front of the wagon was raised up and missing the wheel.

Brody rode where the blacksmith was hammering a new ring on the wagon wheel and dismounted. "Howdy, can I talk to you for a few minutes?"

The man was a short Black man with huge arms and chest. He stopped what he was doing and placed the metal ring onto the bed of coals to heat some more.

"What can I do for you?"

"I'm Brody Connor, and I'm wanting to go south and was wondering if you could tell me what's in that direction."

"My name is Roosevelt, but most folks call me Rosy," said the man, and stuck out his big hand to shake. "How much do you want to know?

"Anything that you can tell me would be great."

"Stay on the Chisholm Trail, and south of here is Little Turkey Creek. You won't have any trouble getting across if you ford it west of where the cattle drives cross. In about eight miles is Dover, another farming community."

"Is there someplace in Dover where a man might rent a room for the night?"

Rosy reached over and gave the bellows a couple of pumps. "I don't rightly know, but I reckon it is, if you ask around when you get there."

Brody moved a couple of steps back from the hot furnace. "What's after Dover?"

"A mile or so is the Cimarron River and again ride upstream until you find a better place to cross. About nine miles south of the river is another town called King-fisher. Kingfisher is a little west of the Chisholm Trail and in the Cheyenne and Arapaho Reservation. The troops from Fort Reno keep watch over the Indians, and you shouldn't have any problems crossing their land."

"Where's Fort Reno located?" asked Brody.

"It's on the south side of the North Canadian River, a mile or so. There's a good-sized town close to the fort where you can buy about anything a man needs in the way of provisions."

Brody stuck out his hand to shake. "Thanks for the information." He turned to leave, but then turned back around. "Did you happen to see a family by the name of Mosley with four wagons pulled by oxen come through here a couple of weeks ago?"

"Can't remember every family that comes by here." Rosy used a pair of tongs to pull the ring off the coals to hammer it in place.

Brody left Hennessey traveling south toward Dover. The creek was easy to cross, and as he came out of the trees that lined both sides of the stream, two men were camped under a huge oak tree. Brody reached down and removed the safety off his gun and stayed ready for battle as he passed by.

Chapter Twenty-Two

THE LAND ALONG THE CHISHOLM TRAIL between Little Turkey Creek and the town of Dover was mostly scrub timber and brush. A few fields had been cleared for farming, and wildlife such as deer and turkey were numerous as Brody took his time and marveled at the landscape.

The faint sound of shooting ignited his senses when he was still a couple of miles from the town. It sounded like more than one gun doing the firing and he wondered if it was coming from a hunting party or was it coming from town.

Not wanting to be taken by surprise, the young traveler removed the safety off both his pistols and for some unknown reason, he began to chew on his bottom lip. Where did this come from? He had never done that before, that he could remember, and continued on into Dover.

It wasn't much of a town, but it did have a few businesses, and one of them was a saloon where the hitching rails were full of tied-up horses. With the number of horses lined up, the first thought that came to mind was, a herd was probably stopped close to town, and the cowhands had come to wash the trail dust down.

The saloon wasn't where Brody had any business at and so he rode on by looking for a place where he could eat a good meal and find a place to sleep. Up ahead was a sign advertising *Hot Food*. The house didn't look like much with its weathered board and shake shingles where some were missing, but it was the only place he saw that had food.

The inside of the house was equipped with tables and chairs in the first two rooms at the front of the house. Brody sat at a table against the wall where he could watch the street and no one could come in behind him. The training from William was working after all.

A young girl of maybe twelve came to the table. "You eating supper?"

Brody replied, "I sure would like to."

"What are you drinking?"

"I'll have water and a plate of whatever you have cooked."

"That'll be chicken, beans, and cornbread," said the girl and started toward a doorway. When Brody turned back to the window, two men were dismounting at the hitch post. He watched them ease their guns up out of the holster an inch and let them fall back into place before the men walked to the door.

Brody pulled the .41 caliber gun from the shoulder holster and laid it in his lap with his hand still gripping the handles. The men came in and took a seat on the far wall, and when the girl came out of the kitchen, one of the men said, "Evening, Sarah, how you doing, honey?"

"I'm okay, Uncle John. Do y'all want coffee to drink?"

"Yeah, and a big plate of food?" replied John.

Brody left the gun in his lap, but put his hand back on the table, waiting on his food. The girl came with his plate and after setting it down she apologized, saying, "I'm sorry, mister. I forgot your water."

"That's quite all right," said Brody, and started eating while she went after his water. The food hit the spot, and with a full belly, the young man was ready to find a place to sleep for the night and decided to ask the girl, and if she didn't know, he would ask the men.

Sarah came to take his plate away when he asked, "Is there someplace where I can rent a room for the night?"

The man called Uncle John butted in and said, "It's not appropriate to ask a young girl about that sort of thing around these parts, mister."

Brody didn't get upset, but he did put his hand back on the pistol that was still in his lap. He looked at Sarah. "I apologize, ma'am." Then he looked at the two men. "It was an innocent question, but I apologized anyway. Do either of you know where I can rent a room for the night?" asked Brody, with a little more confidence in his speech.

John slammed his fork down on the table and pushed his chair back as if he was going to get up. The man's movement instantly caused Brody alarm, and he cocked the hammer back on the gun in his hand.

Brody raised the gun where it could be seen. "John, I don't know what your problem is, but don't even think about getting up and starting something with me. I'm not here for trouble, I just want a place to rest."

John stayed seated, looking at the gun pointed at him. He pointed his index finger at the young man holding the gun on him and said, "We don't want your kind around here, so pay your bill and ride on."

"What do you mean by my kind? You don't know who I am or what I do."

"We see you cowhands come and go all the time and all you do is cause mischief and shoot up the town. We don't want drovers in town going after our women folks, so leave."

Brody pointed the gun barrel toward the floor. "I hate to tell you this, but I'm not a cowboy, I'm a doctor headed south. I don't ride with any herd."

John shook his head like he was disputing what the young man said. "I don't believe you. I think you're lying to save your hide."

Brody wasn't going to be called a liar by some bully with a bad attitude. He stood up, holstered his gun and put four bits on the table before walking to where the two men sat. "Mister, you're a bully and about as dumb as a rock to call someone a liar." Out of nowhere, Brody's fist came around and hit the man with a haymaker that knocked him out of his chair.

John was on his hands and knees when Brody kicked him in the rib cage, knocking the air from his lungs. The other man had gotten up and took one step toward the attacker when Brody went down on one foot and used his other leg to sweep the man's legs out from under him. The man hit the floor so hard that he was knocked unconscious.

John had grabbed hold of the table and was getting up when Brody landed another fist to his chin. It was lights out for John and time for the young man to leave while both men were unconscious.

Dover was one town that he wouldn't spend the night in on this trip, and loped his horse all the way to the Cimarron River. The banks were sloped and muddy where the herds crossed, so he turned upstream and rode another half mile before he urged his horse into the stream and let the animal find his way across.

Darkness was no more than a half hour away and it was time to find a place to camp. Instead of riding south, Brody rode west for another mile before building himself a fire and laying out his bedroll for the night.

The stop in Dover taught him a few things as he pondered on what had happened at the café. His instincts had been right on about the two men, and he had protected himself from a bully. He had also used surprise when landing that first lick and knocking John from the chair. William had taught him the leg sweep, and that came without thinking to take the second man down. In the morning before he leaves camp, he would need to spend time practicing his draw and a few other things the old Indian had taught him.

Chapter Twenty-Three

BRODY WAS UP BY THE CRACK OF DAWN WITH HIS fire blazing and standing off to the side, drawing his gun. The practice William taught him was to draw in different situations like with his back to the target where he drew while turning. Another was on his knees drawing without getting up.

He spent the best part of an hour practicing before he put the skillet on the hot coals to cook bacon with cold biscuits to warm. This meal would last until he could eat at a café while going through Kingfisher.

The sun had been up for almost two hours before Brody rode south to the next town. No more than a mile from his camp came a herd of longhorns heading north. The dust cloud could be seen before he saw the massive animals as they lumbered along, horns hitting horns.

Not wanting to eat the dust from the animals' hooves, Brody veered to the west about a half mile and skirted around the herd. He had often read in dime novels about cattle drives and wondered if he could be a cowboy. Cattle coming into Kansas was big business and the cowboys off a cattle drive frequented Ludwig's tavern on multiple occasions during the summer and fall each year.

Most of them were nice men, but a few seemed to have a chip on their shoulder over something. Those men had certain skills that Brody had never experienced, and he wanted to be able to participate in a cattle drive sometime during his life.

When he had ridden far enough where the sound of bawling cattle couldn't be heard, the young man angled back east toward where the Chisholm Trail cut through the brush and trees. The riding was much easier where the massive beast had trampled down anything that had been growing.

Someone had put a sign on the west side of the trail where a road crossed the wide path. *Kingfisher,* was printed on the sign in black paint and an arrow pointed to the west.

The sun wasn't up to high noon yet, but curiosity got the best of the young traveler, and he headed in the direction of town. The distance was farther then he thought it would be and had to move off the road to let a stagecoach pass. He hoped the stage line had an office in the town, and if they did, it was possible that he could send a letter to his ma in Wichita. Just the aspects of communicating with his ma excited the young man and urged his horse to go faster.

The land he rode through had a lot of mesquite, scrub oak, blackjack, sage grass, bluestem, and buffalo grass. There was still evidence where herds of buffalo had been through here in years past, by the wallows still visible.

The terrain changed abruptly from grass and brush to cultivated fields. Some had corn standing tall, and some were freshly plowed. A little farther down the road were two teams of large horses with men plowing the soil. Another team pulled a piece of equipment with a disk-like thing that was breaking up the clods, and a third team came up behind the second team planting seed.

It was an amazing sight watching the men work the land, and to make matters better, a covered wagon was parked close by. At the wagon were women and children cooking on an open fire for the field hands. Brody waved as he rode by and continued on toward Kingfisher.

The land surrounding Kingfisher happened to be rich farming land in the confluence of Kingfisher Creek and Uncle John's Creek. The Cheyenne and Arapaho Reservation boundary was only a mile or so west of town and that's the reason the stage had a station in town. It was used for the transportation of folks and the mail between Fort Reno, Darlington Indian Agency, and Kingfisher.

Darlington Indian Agency was located along the North Canadian River where the Chisholm Trail intersected with the river. There was even a school for the Indian children at the agency, along with other enterprises for the Indians.

Kingfisher impressed the young man as he rode down the street and turned onto the main north–south street. The town was laid out where the main part of town was on a north–south street. To the east and west were houses, and there were some houses on the south end of town where the start of another community with houses under construction. Looking at the businesses as he rode by were the typical establishments for towns. A hardware store with merchandise like shovels, hoes, and crosscut saws were on display on the porch under the awning.

Two grocery stores were on opposite sides of the street. The store on the east side had the building set back a few more feet and had a much larger covered porch where items were set out on display.

Two cafés were on the same side of the street, and there was the stage line office, next door to the US Post Office. That's where Brody guided his horse to and dismounted.

The postmaster was inside a little office that had twisted bars vertical over the customer window. The lady came to the window, and Brody stepped up and said, "Good morning, ma'am. I'd like to send a letter to my ma in Wichita, but I don't have any paper or a pencil. Can I get what I need from here?"

"I have everything you need right here, young man. That will be five cents for the paper, envelope, and stamp."

"Thank you," said Brody, and paid the woman who had placed the items through the opening on the window.

The postmistress pointed to the north wall. "There's a counter to your left if you want to write the letter in here or you can do it sommers else and bring it back."

"Thank you, I believe I will do it here," said Brody, and went to the counter and started writing. He had to use both sides of the paper to get everything he wanted to say to his mother. When the letter was finished and in the envelope, Brody walked back to the window. "I'm sorry to bother you, but I've never sent a letter before and don't know what to put on the envelope."

"It's no bother, let me show you the correct way to address an envelope," said the lady, and began to point while the young man wrote. When he was finished and the lady was putting the envelope in a large mail bag that would go on the evening stage, Brody said, "I'll be expecting a reply from my ma. I'm not sure how long I'll be here and was wondering if you would hold my letter until I can come back. I'll be going to Fort Reno, but can ride back once a week to check on the reply."

"I'll keep your mail until you get back."

"Thanks, ma'am, would you mind telling me your name? I'm Brody Connor and training to be a doctor."

"I'm Lucille Walters, and it's nice meeting you Dr. Connor."

"Just call me Brody. I'm not a full-fledged doctor yet," said the boy, and turned to leave.

"You probably don't know this, but our town doctor left three months ago, heading home to Virginia to care for a sick relative, and we ain't had a doctor since. His office is down the street and should have everything a doctor needs to work. All he took with him was a clothing satchel," said Lucille.

"Thanks for the help and the information, Lucille. I'll check out the doctor's office while I'm here." Brody walked outside.

The information about the doctor's office intrigued the young man but he would prefer to speak with someone with authority before he went to the place and went inside. That could be seen as him breaking in, and he didn't need any more lawmen after him. It was close enough to noon, so he decided to eat and find out more about the town.

Chapter Twenty-Four

TYING THE HORSE TO THE HITCH RAIL CLOSE TO the café and stepping onto the boardwalk, the young man changed his mind about eating and walked past a few businesses to the hotel.

The interior of the hotel wasn't fancy or elaborate as the stranger walked to the counter. "Good day, sir. Does the hotel have baths in the rooms?"

"Yes, sir, five of our rooms have bathtubs for your bathing pleasure. That will be three dollars a night and that includes hot water for the bath."

Brody turned his back to the man so he couldn't see his money, and when he turned back, he laid the cash on the countertop. "I'll take one of those rooms with a bath and will need it in one hour if that's enough time."

"Your bath will be ready in one hour and here's the key to room seven on the second floor. This floor is the dining room and our living arrangements. If you would like to eat with us tonight, my wife fixes some mighty fine food for only two dollars a plate," said the man, grinning.

Brody touched the brim of his hat. "I'll let you know." He turned and started up the stairs to his room. Two dollars a plate seemed a little expensive, but that could be the going rate in Kingfisher. The room was small on the inside of the hall without any windows, but it did have a bathtub, chair, nightstand, and of course a bed. This would be the first real bath he had had in over a month, and looking in the mirror revealed that he needed a shave and haircut. The clothes in the travel bag were sort of clean, they had been washed in creek water and at the time that was clean enough.

The hotel clerk said the bath would be ready in an hour and that would give him time to walk to one of the clothing stores and buy some new duds to wear. Brody didn't lock the room door and walked to the clothing store, where he purchased britches, a shirt, socks, and long underwear.

Brody counted out the money to pay for his purchase and asked, "Is there someplace in town where I can have my clothes washed?"

"There's a woman by the name of Rosalie two streets to the west, on the corner in a house with a porch swing. It's the house with a fence. She does laundry and ironing for folks," said the store salesperson.

Brody placed his package under his left arm. "Thanks." He remembered his training to not carry anything on his gun side.

The young man scrubbed the dirt and grime from the past month off and then got out and dressed in his new clothes. He stuffed all his soiled clothes in his bag and left to see Rosalie.

Brody walked up to the door and read the message attached to the screen door. *Come to the backyard*. He walked around the house to the backyard to find a large wash shed with three piles of soiled clothes on the wooden floor. Rosalie was much younger than he antici-pated and was a little embarrassed that he had brought such a young woman his dirty underclothes.

"Howdy, ma'am, I'm Brody Connor, and I was told at the store that you might wash my clothes."

She stopped what she was doing and came to him and stuck out a soapy hand. She saw the suds on her hand and pulled it back to wipe them away on the apron covering the front of her dress.

It's nice to meet you, Brody. Just make a pile over there and I'll get to them later. Do you want them ironed as well?"

Brody nodded and smiled. "That would be nice. I've been on the trail for some time and ironed clothes would be wonderful."

"You can come by tomorrow afternoon and pick up your clothes. By the way, I'm Betsy. My ma is Rosalie."

Brody grinned and being a little love-struck, said, "I was wondering about that. How old are you, Miss Betsy?"

"You know it's not nice to ask a girl her age, but since I want to know yours also, I'm seventeen. How old are you, Brody Connor?"

"I'll be nineteen in two weeks. I'm passing through, trying to find a place where I can study to be a doctor. I've been a doctor's assistant for two years and I want to help people."

"I reckon you know that Dr. Stevens's office is vacant and we ain't had a doctor here in three months or more. You may want to take his office over and stay awhile. I would be glad to show you around the town so folks could meet you."

"I heard that the doctor was gone and I intend to go

look his office over, but I wanted to get in clean clothes, get a shave and haircut before I went there." He dumped his clothes on the floor. "Do you work for your ma all the time, or would you be available to help me clean the doctor's office if I decide to stay?"

The girl took him by surprise and walked over and took his hand into hers. "All you have to do is come calling and I'll be more than glad to work for you, Dr. Brody. I may even teach you a few things in the process." She went back to the washtub to continue her work.

Brody's face turned red, and he gathered up enough nerve to reply. "I may teach you a few things also, and if you hadn't walked away just now, I might have kissed you."

The back screen door on the house slammed, and Brody turned to see Rosalie coming to the wash shed. It was time to make an exit before this got out of hand. Brody turned to the woman and said, "I'm Brody Connor and new to Kingfisher. I'm thinking about taking over the doctor's office and helping folks."

Rosalie smiled. "I see, and does that include courting my only daughter?"

Brody was taken by surprise again, but the lady started laughing. "It's nice to meet you Brody, and I was only joshing you."

"I knew that," said Brody, still embarrassed and then turned to Betsy. "I'll be back tomorrow for my clothes."

He then stuck out his hand to Rosalie. "It's nice meeting you, Miss Rosalie, and I think your daughter is mighty pretty." He walked off without saying anything else, but had a smile on his face all the way back to Main Street.

The barber shop had five men sitting in chairs and the barber sitting in his chair. When Brody came inside, the barber got up and said, "Young man, sit down and I'll get busy while you catch up on all the town's gossip from these old coots."

Brody took off his hat and hung it on the hat tree along with his vest. He could see the men eyeing the shoulder gun, but none of them said anything about it. The barber went to work on the hair with scissors and a comb. While trimming off the hair, the barber asked, "Are you wanting a shave also when I'm through with the hair?"

"Yes, sir, it's been a while since I had a good shave."

He didn't pay any attention to the five men who were talking, laughing, and cutting up with each other. Then one of the men asked, "Young man, are you the new doctor in town?"

Brody thought about his answer for a few seconds before he answered. "I'm Brody Connor, and I'm studying to be a doctor. I haven't made up my mind if I want to stay or ride on. I've heard that the doctor has left and the office is vacant, but I don't know who to talk to about using it if I stay."

"That's the easiest thing you can do. You see, I'm Lucas Waverley and I'm the mayor of our little city, and if you'll stay, then the office is yours to use."

"I appreciate that, Lucas. Who are the men you're sitting with?"

"Feller on the end is John Johnson and next to him is Willie Hammersmith. This old coot on my right is Rily Green, and on the other side of him is David Jones."

Brody made a little wave with his left hand. "Nice to meet all of you."

The barber spoke up and said, "I'm George McGovern. I'm one of the first settlers to come to live at Kingfisher."

"It's nice to meet you, also George, especially since you're about to shave my pretty face with that straight razor."

The men laughed at Brody's remark, and the talk continued until he paid the barber and walked outside.

Chapter Twenty-Five

THE LOCATION OF THE SUN HAD DRIFTED overhead, and Brody decided to have dinner before he went to the doctor's office to check it out. The young man hoped the doctor had lots of books he could study while in town. The more he learns, the easier medical school will be when he attends classes.

Most of the tables in the diner were occupied with locals at noon time. This eating establishment had a long bar with stools where individuals could belly up to the counter and eat. Brody found an open stool and asked the man sitting next to it, "Sir, is this seat taken?"

"No, sir, Doctor. Have a seat. I'm Bartholemew Krum." The man stuck out his hand.

Brody shook the man's hand. "Thanks, I'm Brody Connor."

Brody carried on a conversation with his new acquaintance until the man finished his food and stood up to leave. "It's been my pleasure talking to you, son. I'm one of the owners of the feed store and have to get back to work now."

Brody had to swallow a mouthful of food before he could talk. "It was nice meeting you, sir. Maybe I'll see you around town."

Brody left the diner, and his curiosity got the best of him. He had to see inside the doctor's office with the hopes of finding books to study. As he made his way down the boardwalk, five cowboys came down the street galloping their horses. Townspeople scrambled to get out of the way, and some of them hollered out to the men who finally stopped in front of the saloon. They were most likely with a herd heading north or on their way home from a trail drive and wanted to kick up their heels and have whiskey to wash down the trail dust.

It seemed like the local town marshal would come out and stop the drovers from running their horses down the busy city streets. Brody could see where innocent folks could get hurt from the misbehaving men.

The door wouldn't open when Brody tried to open it. It had been suggested by a few of the town folks that the door may not be locked. Where could the key be hidden if the doctor had left it behind? He felt over the top of the door frame and didn't find anything but dust. The most obvious place was under a mat that people used to wipe off the bottom of their footwear, but that was too obvious. No one would hide a key there. He raised the mat, and sure enough, the key was there.

The key worked and the door screeched as it came open. The hinges needed a good oiling, but that could be how he knew if someone came in. The only light in the room was from the open door. Brody went to the windows and opened the curtains, and dust coming off them clouded the room. He continued to open curtains and windows for the fresh air. The place had a musty smell in it.

What he found while opening windows was a small reception space. A hallway, which took him to an examining room, and an operating room on the right. Across the hall on the left was a larger room with four beds for patients. A door at the end of the hall opened into the doctor's private residence which was one room that served as a living room and kitchen. In another room was the bedroom.

The kitchen had a door that opened outside where the doctor had a vegetable garden, where there were still a few tomatoes, peas, and onions growing.

Against the outside wall was what looked like four ricks of wood and two washtubs hanging on the wall. After more observation, he saw a water well close to the garden and toward the back alley was the outhouse. It looked like everything he would need while in Kingfisher was here.

Brody went back inside and spent more time in each room trying to figure out where to start and decided to start in the living quarters. He could get it clean and the bedding washed so he could move into it tomorrow.

With a fire built in the wood cookstove and two buckets of water heating, the young man got busy stripping the covers off the bed and taking them outside to one of the washtubs. After washing the bedding, he hung it on the clothesline to dry.

With the bedding washed and drying, the next thing was dusting, sweeping, and wiping down everything with a damp rag. The room took shape quicker than he thought it would and went to the reception area next. He shook out the dust from the curtains and then cleaned off all the furniture before he swept the floor.

With darkness only an hour away, Brody filled the lamps with kerosene so he could work a few more hours before going to the hotel. Three hours after dark, the young man locked the door and headed to the café for supper where he was the only one there at this time of night.

At the hotel, he went to bed without taking off his clothes. Today had been more work than he had ever done and was so tired that it was daylight when he woke up.

————

BREAKFAST WAS TAKEN at the diner he had used the day before and most of the people inside greeted him as *Doctor*. Brody briefly talked to a few that he had seen the day before.

He thought about what he would do today as he opened the door and went inside. In the examining room as well as the operating room were vertical cabinets with glass doors. Inside the cabinets were various instruments, and on one shelf were bottles of medicine.

Those instruments lying inside the cabinet would need to be sterilized before they could be used. The examination room would be first to get started on, and with all the instruments gathered up and placed in a large pot of boiling water, he started thinking how he could store them without getting them contaminated.

There was nothing in the office, so he went to the hardware store and purchased a few bread pans and bottles of rubbing alcohol. With the containers clean and the sterilized instruments in the pans covered in alcohol. He laid clean rags over the pans and placed them back into the cabinets.

The medicine bottles in the examination room contained laudanum and chloroform. The last shelf contained rolls of gauze and stacks of square bandages in different sizes. Brody sat on the examination table and thought about how fortunate he was to have such a great place to practice being a doctor.

The last room was the operating room where he sterilized all the instruments and placed them in alcohol pans. The operating room, along with the patients' beds needed to have all the sheets washed but that was more than he wanted to do right now.

Time had flown by working in the office, and he remembered that he should go get his clothes from Betsy. He smiled at the thought of the pretty girl and dusted off his clothes and headed out the door.

Again, the paper was attached to the door, and he went around back to find the girl folding the last of a load of clothes on the worktable. She looked up and motioned with her hand for him to come inside. When he was near, she pointed to her left and said, "Go stand over there while I finish up."

"And good afternoon to you, too," said Brody.

He hadn't no more than got the words out of his mouth until the girl was in front of him and kissed him on the lips. It was a quick kiss but then she did it again, and it lasted longer this time. "Is that better than saying good afternoon?" she asked, giggling.

Grinning from ear to ear. "It sure is." He couldn't believe his good fortune. "Do you have my clothes ready?"

"Yes, I do. They're over there." She pointed to a bundle of clothing. "Brody, do you need me to come and help you get set up in the doctor's office this afternoon"?

Brody took a step toward his clothes. "If it's not too much trouble. If you can, let's go have dinner and then we can work on the office."

"I think that's a marvelous idea. "She went to the door and called out to her ma. Rosalie came to the door with a broom in her hand. "Hello, Doctor. What do you want, Betsy?"

"Brody has asked me to have dinner and then work for him in his office, getting it ready for patients. I won't be back by supper, but I'll be here by bedtime," said Betsy, and pulled the apron over her head and laid it on the worktable.

"Do you have everything finished out here or do I need to do something?" asked her ma.

"No, it's all done, and Brody will pay me for his laundry."

"You kids have fun and don't be out late."

Brody looked at Rosalie. "I'll take good care of her," and the two walked off.

Chapter Twenty-Six

BRODY FOUND OUT OVER DINNER THAT BETSY'S pa had died in a farming accident, and after his death, Rosalie rented out the section of farmland they owned south of Kingfisher. Betsy and her mom started the laundry and ironing business to have something to do, plus earn extra income.

Betsy had also completed the twelfth grade that year and had no plans for the future. She was satisfied living with her ma and working in the wash shed.

When the two young people stepped out of the diner, Betsy reached down and put her hand in Brody's. She commenced to walk beside him holding onto his hand. Brody didn't know what to think, since he had never had a girlfriend before.

They were almost to the doctor's office when Betsy pointed to the front of the building. "You need a new sign on the doctor's office."

"It really doesn't belong to me, but I could put my name under Dr. Stevens's name, I reckon."

Suddenly, they heard hollering from up the street,

and one of the saloon girls was coming toward them, waving her arms, crying and hollering for help.

Betsy stopped Brody from walking. "What in the world is wrong with that floozy?"

"I don't know," said Brody, and started out into the street pulling Betsy along. "Come on, let's see what's wrong."

The saloon girl had blood on her dress, hands, and arms as she was met by the young couple. Brody spoke in a concerned voice. "What's the matter?"

"Doctor, come quick. Someone has almost killed Emeral," said the woman while sucking in a gasp of air.

Brody didn't think to grab the black bag he found in the office. His first instinct was to go to the woman and see what the injury was. The three of them ran to the saloon where an uproar seemed to be engaged on the far side of the room. Brody, Betsy, and the saloon girl rushed upstairs where three more girls were standing in the hallway crying.

Brody rushed through the bedroom door to find the woman on the bed naked and covered in blood. It was a sight he had seen many times in his life, and the anger boiled his blood. The poor woman had been beaten so bad that her face was a bloody pulp. There were bruises the size of a man's fist on her breast, stomach, and rib cage. By the initial look of the bruises, the man had stomped her with his booted foot. Both legs were badly bruised and then he noticed the blood on her abdomen. It was coming from what looked like stab wounds or cuts in the area of her breast.

An elderly Black man came into the room and put his hand to his cheek. "Oh lord. He done beat Miss Emeral to a pulp. Is she alive?"

Brody bent down and felt to see if she had a pulse.

"Yeah, she's alive, but we have to move her to my office down the street. I don't know if I can save her life, but I want to try."

"Yes, sir." The man motioned to the girls. "You girls get your tails in here and give us a hand."

Brody pointed to the patient. "Leave her on the quilt and we'll use it like a stretcher. I don't want to move her no more than necessary until I've had time to thoroughly make my examination."

Two more men came in, and the Black man directed them on how to carry her down the stairs. One of the saloon girls in the room had a scared look on her face. "It may be better to take her down the outside stairway. Harris Chumbley is still in the saloon, drunk and crazy mad. He's libel to start shooting if he sees us with Emeral."

Brody pointed to the door. "Ma'am, you lead the way and I'll bring up the rear."

As the men took off with the woman, Brody took Betsy by her arm. "I'd appreciate it if you would come to the office and help me. I'm a little concerned about the man that did this, so I'm going to hang back. I want you to run on ahead and open the door and have them put her on the examination table."

"I'll help, but I want to stay back with you."

Brody was shaking his head. "No! If the man comes for her or us, then I'm going to do what I have to do and it may not be nice. Run on to the office."

Betsy hadn't even made it across the street when the man they had called Harris came out of the saloon with his gun in his hand, cursing and shouting obscenities at Brody and the other men carrying the girl.

Brody stopped in the street. "You men keep going and get her inside. I'll see to Harris."

Brody turned to the saloon and walked a few steps south where the sun was too his back. He had his bottom lip in his teeth as he removed the safeties off both his guns and stood waiting until Harris came within twelve feet of him.

Brody stuck up his left hand. "Harris, never again will you beat that girl or any woman in this town. If you come any closer, you'd better be ready to pay for your sins."

The man started laughing with his gun still in his hand, pointed toward the ground. "Boy, you ain't no match for me. I already have my gun out, now move aside or I'll kill you right here."

Brody looked Harris in the eyes and never flinched. "Raise your gun when you're ready to die." The young man stood his ground and was biting his lip when Harris made a growling noise and raised the gun.

Brody pulled his gun faster than he even thought he could. He was firing at the man with his pistol waist high as the man pulled back the hammer on his gun and fired into the ground. Harris went to his knees and made the growling sound again while trying to bring up his gun when Brody fired one more time with another bullet to his chest. Harris tumbled over face down in the dirt street, dead.

Brody stood watching the man while he reloaded his gun. He looked over at the saloon to make sure none of Harris's friends wanted in on the fight. With his pistol reloaded, but still in his hand. He kneeled beside Harris and put his hand on the man's neck to see if he was still alive. Unfortunately for Harris, he was dead.

Brody got up to go check on his patient when Betsy came running up to him crying and put her arms around his neck. "I was so scared he would kill you. I had no idea you were a gunslinger as well as a doctor."

Brody took in a huge breath of air and let it out. "The truth is, I didn't know it either. That's the first time I've ever done that. Let's go examine the patient, Nurse Betsy."

They were almost to the porch of the doctor's office when someone called out, "Hold up, mister. I need a word with you."

Brody turned to see a man in his sixties, medium height with a pot belly coming toward him. The man had a tin star pinned to his vest and was sweating up a storm from walking fast.

Brody looked at the man and waved him off with his hand. "I don't have time for you now. I have to examine the girl who was beaten by that man in the street. You can come by later today or tomorrow." He took Betsy's hand and went inside, leaving the town marshal with a dumbfounded look on his face.

Chapter Twenty-Seven

THE MEN FROM THE SALOON HAD CARRIED HIS patient into the examining room and left her with the two girls that came with them. Brody came into the room. "Thanks, men. You can go back to the saloon now." He continued to the narrow bed where the unconscious woman lay.

Brody started rolling up the sleeves of his shirt. "Betsy, would you mind going into the kitchen and getting a fire going? Also, get two large pans of water boiling, then come back in here."

Brody stood beside the bloodied patient. "Ladies, keep her still while I wash my hands."

He went into the kitchen and scrubbed his hands with lye soap and then poured alcohol over them with Betsy watching in awe of what he was doing. With his hands clean, Brody began to examine the places that were still seeping blood. Then he started at her head and said to the two girls still with him, "Her nose is broken and to the side. Hold her down while I put it back in place. This is going to hurt." With that, he placed both hands on the woman's face and shoved the nose back in place. She let out a scream and almost came off the table before slumping back down.

Betsy came in to see what had happened. "The water is almost boiling, Doctor."

Brody pointed to the cabinet where he had towels. "Go into the kitchen and wash your hands with soap. Then pour alcohol over them. After that, get one towel out of that cabinet and wet it with the boiling water. Better yet, bring the pot of water and the wash pan in here. I want you to start cleaning the blood off this poor woman so we can see all the damage."

Brody went to work disinfecting and sewing up the cut wounds while Betsy cleaned the woman's face, arms, and legs. When Brody was finished putting in stitches, he told the saloon girls they could leave.

"Betsy, go ahead and wash off her chest and stomach while I look for some Arnica Tincture Liniment to put on the bruises." Brody hadn't seen any earlier and had to look in the operating room cabinet to finally find it.

He brought the jar of ointment in and handed it to Betsy. "Would you rub some of this liniment on her breast and stomach while I do the legs? Then we can move her to a bed and cover up her nakedness."

Emeral was still lying on the quilt that the men had used as a stretcher. With the help of Betsy, the two of them were able to raise the hurt woman up enough where Betsy could wash her back and apply liniment to the bruises on her back and backside.

Emeral started to open and close her eyes and moan as she regained consciousness. "Take it slow, Emeral. I'm Dr. Brody and you're in my office getting treated."

"Can I have water?"

Brody looked at Betsy. "You stay with her and I'll get the water and something for her pain."

He returned with a glass of water and then gave her laudanum for the pain. "Emeral, we need to move you into the other room and get you in a bed. Do you think you can help us by walking?"

"I can try. I hurt all over, and I'm sick to my stomach."

With Betsy on one side and Brody on the other, they were able to get Emeral into bed and covered up. With another spoonful of the pain medication, she went to sleep, and Brody took Betsy by the hand and took her back to the examination room.

Betsy sat down in one of the two chairs and slumped down. "Brody, this has been some day. I watched you in a gunfight where you killed a man and then I watched you come in here and save that woman's life."

"Truthfully, I didn't know I had it in me to face Harris. But I have to tell you something about me that's not nice. My stepfather beat me and my ma for years. A few months ago, I came home to find her on the floor in a pool of blood, beaten again. I decided when I saw her that never again would he ever beat her. I took a gun and went to the man's tavern with the intention of shooting him, but I tripped on a chair leg and the gun went off. The bullet hit him in the head, and I ran. That's how I ended up here. I don't know if the law is after me or not, but I do know that two men have been looking for me."

Betsy sat with her mouth wide open, listening to his story. "Brody, do you think those men will come here looking for you?"

"I don't know. I've given it a lot of thought and I'm

135

not going to run from them. Even though I shot Ludwig by accident, I went there that day to kill him. I sent my ma a letter and I'm waiting to hear back from her. I understand if you don't want to see me anymore since you know my past."

Betsy got up and walked over to Brody. She put a hand on his shoulder and walked around his chair, and when she was standing in front of him, she leaned over and kissed his lips. "I've decided to give you a second chance, that is if you agree," she said, and sat on his lap for more kissing.

Brody finally broke the kiss and said, "It may not look very professional if someone comes into the office and finds the nurse and doctor kissing."

"Do you really care what people think?" asked Betsy, and kissed him again.

"We should probably clean up in here in case someone else needs help," said Brody.

"You're probably right," said Betsy, and got up after one more kiss. The two of them cleaned up the table and the tools he used treating Emeral. When they were finally finished, Brody pointed to the door where Emeral was. "Let's see how the patient is doing and then we can go to the diner for supper. By looking out the window, I'd say it's getting about dark."

"That sounds good to me," said Betsy. "You check on Emeral and I'll go in your bedroom and touch up a bit before we go out in public."

Brody and Betsy enjoyed a good meal, and Betsy ordered a cup of coffee to settle the food. While she was sipping the coffee, two men came in, and something told Brody that these men were trouble. He reached inside his vest and removed the safety off the gun in the shoulder holster. The men sat off to the side where they were not in clear sight. Brody adjusted the chair where he could watch them. Betsy came aware of what her date was doing and touched his hand, "I'm finished and ready to leave if you are."

Brody reached out with his left hand and took her hand into his. He pulled her closer and said quietly. "Get up and go outside in front of me. Those men may be trouble."

Betsy got up and was almost to the door when Brody stood up, but turned where the men couldn't see his hand inside his vest and walked to the door. He kept his hand on the gun handle as he and Betsy started across the street. Brody watched the light from the windows, and when he saw shadows, he turned loose of Betsy's hand and said, "Run to your left. Now!"

Brody turned around in time to see the men pulling their guns. The young man pulled the shoulder gun and was firing as the men started to fire. Both men were hit and going to the ground. They were still firing their guns, but the bullets were going into the dirt.

Brody holstered the shoulder gun and pulled the one on his hip as he walked up to the men. One was already dead, but the other one was still alive.

"Why did you come after me?" asked Brody as Betsy came sobbing and stood by his side. Two other men who were in the diner having supper, also came outside.

"We worked with Harris on the cattle drive. He was our friend," said the man choking on his blood.

Brody holstered his gun. "I reckon it takes being a good friend to give your life for someone who beats women."

The town marshal came running up, out of breath and covered in sweat. "Mister, you ain't been in town three days and done killed three men."

Brody looked at the lawman with contempt in his expression. "I reckon the law needs to work a little harder to keep the criminals out. All these people are witnesses to why these two tried to shoot me in the back. Maybe you should ask the good citizens from the diner what happened."

"I'll do just that," said the lawman. "Miss Betsy, did you see what happened?"

"I sure did, Lonnie. They followed us out of the diner and was going to shoot us because they were friends of that woman-beater that got killed earlier. You should be ashamed for blaming the doctor for shooting this trash."

The lawman shot back at her. "I ain't blaming him. I just want to know the truth."

Betsy put her hands on her hips. "Well, you know it now. Come on, Doctor, let's go check on our patient."

She took Brody by the hand, but he stopped her. "I have to check on this man to see if I can help him." He kneeled down beside the injured man and checked to see if he was still alive. Shaking his head, he got up and took Betsy's hand.

They walked back inside the office, and Brody went to check on his patient. She was still sleeping but the cover had slid down, exposing her nakedness. Brody covered her back up then went to find Betsy.

"Betsy, we need to walk to the saloon and have one of the girls get something for Emeral to wear. I don't like her in there with no clothes on."

Betsy was shaking her head up and down. "I agree, I don't want you looking at that hussy." She took his hand in hers and they took off.

One of the saloon girls found a gown, and when they returned to the doctor's office, Betsy went in to put it on Emeral.

When she returned to the living room where Brody sat, she said, "I bet you're tired from all the excitement of the day. It's after dark, and I should be going home unless you want me to stay."

Brody stood up and put on his hat. "I'll walk you home so the boogeyman don't get you."

Chapter Twenty-Eight

KINGFISHER'S DANCE HALL AND THE TWO saloons were in full swing with piano music filtering out of the establishments as Brody and Betsy walked by holding hands. No more than a block from Betsy's house, she stopped and faced Brody. "I would have spent the night with you if you had asked."

That took Brody by surprise, and it was a good thing it was dark out, his face was so red from the thought of intimacy. "I'm not ready for that, Betsy," said Brody, stammering out the words.

"Now don't get the wrong idea about me. I've never been with a boy that way either. I know in my heart that it'll be you when that time comes." She pulled on his hand and started walking off.

At the house, Betsy put her arms around Brody's neck and kissed him for a long time. "I think today was the most interesting date a girl could have. You keep your eyes off that hussy from the saloon."

Again, Brody was taken by surprise by what she said about his patient. "I certainly will," stammered Brody.

"Can I come see you tomorrow when my work is finished?" she asked.

"Of course. I would love to see you tomorrow."

They kissed one more time and Betsy went inside.

Brody had the girl on his mind as he strolled back toward the office where he would sleep tonight. He thought about his clothes and remembered that they were still at the hotel and would need to fetch them before they were put in the trash.

Walking through town in the dark revealed a concern for the practicing doctor. There was coughing coming from more than a few houses and that most likely meant that the cold was going around. If that was the case, he would start seeing a lot of patients soon and didn't remember seeing anything in the office to fight it with.

After picking up his bag from the hotel and taking it back to the office, he checked on Emeral, who was awake and hungry. That was something else the young doctor hadn't thought about. Food would need to be prepared for his in-house patients and that wasn't something he could do. After being on his own the last few months, cooking was not one of his strong points. Maybe Betsy would hire on to cook food when there were patients staying at the office.

Brody was hoping the diner would still have some food left and started that way only to be stopped by a man in a wagon.

"Doctor, I'm Alex Winters, and my wife and kids are sick at home. I was wondering if you could ride out to my place and doctor them?"

"Hello Alex, I'm Brody Connor. Can you describe their conditions?"

"They're coughing, runny nose, and hacking up stuff. My wife and kids can't sleep for coughing."

"I'm going after food for a patient that's in a bed in my office right now. Where exactly do you live?"

"Well, I'm about three south and two east and then south a half. It's a little hard to find if a person ain't never been there before. How about I wait on you and you can follow me out there?"

"I can do that, but it'll be about an hour before I can be ready to go."

The man looked around and pointed toward the saloon. "I'll be in the saloon when you're ready." He slapped the reins on the horse and started off.

Brody happened to turn toward the saloon as the man was getting down and as he put his booted foot in the wagon spoke as a step, the first thing the young doctor saw was the spurs on the man's heels.

Brody stepped in between the diner and another building so the shadow would conceal him. The man wore a gun in a tied-down holster, and he didn't set the brake on the wagon.

When Alex or whoever he was, went inside the saloon, Brody went into the diner.

The waitress looked up when the door closed. "Hello, Doctor, are you hungry already?"

"No, but I need food for Emeral. She's awake and hungry. Do you have any soup or stew?"

"I may have stew left. Let me go see."

Brody sat down and was still thinking about this Alex person when the girl came back.

"Mama is heating up the stew and cornbread. Can I get you a cup of coffee while you wait?"

"No, I don't drink coffee, but I would like to ask you about a man by the name of Alex Winters."

The girl shook her head. "I don't know anyone by that name."

The woman from the kitchen came out with a bowl covered by a plate. "Here's the food. You can bring my dishes back tomorrow."

"Thanks, ma'am. I sure do appreciate it," he said, and he handed her money for the food. The girl spoke to her ma. "Do you know who Alex Winters is?"

"Nope, never heard of him. Why do you ask?"

Brody chimed in, "A man stopped me on the street while I was walking here. He was in that wagon parked in front of the saloon, and said he was Alex Winters. That feller said his family was sick and wants me to doctor them. I'm supposed to follow him to his farm which is about three south and two east and then south a half."

"That don't seem right. Two east would put you on Samson Hider's land. Old Samson owns like four or five sections out there, and I guarantee you that he ain't letting no one live on his property with all the kids of his working the land. He has seven boys and five girls that work like mules all day long."

"Thanks for the food and the information. You all have a good night," said Brody, and left the diner.

The wagon was still parked in front of the saloon, and the young doctor had to make an important decision on what he would do. A part of him wanted to believe the man about his family being sick. But another part of him thought too many red flags were going up to believe the man.

Brody took the food to his office, and with his help, Emeral was able to sit up and eat most of the stew. When she was finished and lying back down, Brody set the plate aside and sat down.

"Emeral, if you're still feeling better tomorrow and your wounds are showing signs of healing, I believe that you can go back to your room at the saloon. I'll have some instructions on what you can do in the way of working."

"Thank you, Dr. Brody. I sure do appreciate you, and if there's ever anything you need, you let me know," said Emeral, tilting her head to the side and smiling.

"I'm sure you will, Miss Emeral. Do you know a man by the name of Alex Winters?"

She thought for a moment. "I don't know anyone by that name."

"I'll be back later," said Brody, and went out, but this time he left by way of the back door and made his way to the other saloon south of his office and went inside. He saw a few faces that he recognized and nodded to the men as he made his way to the bar's countertop.

The barkeep came over. "What can I get you, Doctor?"

"I'd like a bottle of whiskey that I can make into cough medicine, and I'd like to know if you know a man by the name of Alex Winters."

"Alex Winters ain't a name I'm familiar with." Then he bellowed, "Anyone know a man by the name of Alex Winters?" The men were shaking their heads no, and the barkeep went after the whiskey.

He brought the bottle and set it on the counter. "I normally charge two dollars for a bottle, but since you're using it for medicine, I only want one dollar."

Brody laid the money on the counter. "I appreciate that. What's your name?"

"Everyone calls me Mac."

"Thanks, Mac, and it was nice meeting you." Brody walked out with his bottle. Back on the boardwalk, he removed the safety off his gun with a fear that he could get bushwhacked walking at night. No one knew who

Alex was and that was beginning to really make him think the man was up to something.

The grocery store happened to still be open, but he could tell that the owner was doing the final preparations to open in the morning. "Sir, would you happen to have a jar of honey and maybe something with lemon in it?" asked Brody.

The store owner set his broom against the counter. "It sounds like you're going to make a toddy for the cold. I have honey down that second aisle and over by the counter is some Salem Gibraltar that's used for the sore throat. I'm sure it has some lemon in the ingredients."

"That'll work wonderfully. By the way, what's your name?" asked Brody.

The man stuck out his hand. "It's Mitchel Womack, and I believe you're the new Dr. Brody that's in Dr. Steven's office."

"Yes, sir, I am, and it's nice meeting you." Brody got what he came for and headed back to his office.

Chapter Twenty-Nine

BRODY WALKED DOWN THE STREET CARRYING the bottle of whiskey, honey, and the hard candy on his way to the saloon. Dirt and grime covered most of the large windows on the front of the building, but Brody could see enough to make out Alex. He was sitting at one of the poker tables playing cards and drinking whiskey with three other men.

Knowing that Alex was occupied, Brody walked to the office where he heated together the whiskey, honey, and ground-up candy. There were small empty bottles in one of the cabinets that he used to fill five bottles.

Emeral was asleep when he looked in on her, and with one of the bottles in his pocket, he left through the back door again.

Time was of the essence, and he didn't want Alex to come looking for him until he had his horse saddled. At the stable, the hostler was mucking stalls and came to Brody.

"Evening, Doctor. Do you need your horse?"

"Yes, could you saddle him up and leave him tied outside while I go run an errand?"

"I sure will," said the man, and started to one of the stalls.

Brody walked back to the saloon, and when he stepped inside, William's training took over, and he stood until his eyes adjusted to the light. Alex rose from his chair and grabbed his money. Brody waited on the man and followed him outside.

"I brought you medicine for your sick family. Each of them can take a tablespoon as needed for the cough," said Brody, and handed the man the bottle.

Alex looked at the bottle. "Ain't you going to examine them? I really would like for you to follow me to my place so you can see how sick they are."

"I'm sorry, but I have a patient in my office that's in real bad shape and I can't leave her tonight. You take this with you and if they ain't better by day after tomorrow, you come get me."

Brody could tell the man was perturbed at him by the tone of his voice and how fidgety he was getting. "You go on home and start them on that medicine tonight." Brody backed away while biting his lower lip, never taking his eyes off of Alex.

The doctor was halfway across the street when he turned and rushed to his office. When he looked back, Alex was in the wagon seat, turning the rig around to leave.

Brody went inside the office and on through the back door and briskly walked to the livery and mounted up. The dark shape of the wagon could still be seen as the young doctor followed after it. Brody knew the man was trying to set a trap, but he didn't know why unless he was a bounty hunter.

Three miles south of town, the wagon turned east, and Brody turned where he was and rode at an angle across a field of corn that hadn't been harvested. Up ahead sat the wagon and three horses with men on two of the mounts. It was too dark to see the men's faces. He dismounted and walked bent over so he could get close enough to hear their conversation.

Alex was talking. "I think he knows something was going to happen. That doctor is smarter than we thought. When he handed me the medicine, he backed all the way to the middle of the street."

"What're we going to do now?" asked one of the men.

Alex spit on the ground. "We all know how mean Harris was to women. I reckon he beat the wrong one, and from what I heard in the saloon, that doctor is mighty fast with a gun. I vote we leave here and head on home. Harris ain't worth getting killed over."

One of the other two men spoke, "I agree with Alex. Let's ride and get on home. What're you going to do with this wagon you stole?"

We'll leave it on the road. Someone will find it tomorrow," said Alex, and rode to the horses pulling the wagon and led them back to the road.

Brody stayed put until he couldn't hear the men anymore as they rode south. This turned out good, and no one had to get hurt or be killed. It was time to go back to town and get some rest.

Emeral was awake when Brody arrived back at the doctor's office. She was not only awake but sitting at his kitchen table, drinking coffee and playing cards.

Brody came in and put his hat on the table. "Well, it seems like you're doing better."

"Yeah, Henderson, my boss at the saloon visited me

and I told him what you said about me being limited on what I could do. He said that I could deal cards for a few weeks until I was back to normal. I wish there was something we could do to make my black eyes go away," said Emeral.

He looked closer to her eyes. "They're already losing some of the color. Give it another week, and most of the swelling and discoloration will be gone." He pulled out a chair and sat down. "Teach me how to play cards."

Brody and Emeral sat at the table for two hours playing five-card stud, and five-card draw. When Brody finally threw in his cards and pushed away from the table, he said, "It's been fun and I appreciate you teaching me about cards, but I'm tired and need my rest."

"I'm ready to go to sleep too. You did good learning to play, and I suggest you come to the saloon and play sometime."

Brody lay awake for a long time thinking about his future. The two men looking for him were still out there somewhere, and that could be a setback. Betsy was a nice girl, and he could see her as his girlfriend, but that could be a problem if those men came here looking for him.

It was a good thing that he had enough suspicion about Alex to ask around town before he rode off with the man. Revenge over the death of their friend had blinded the man until his friends said that Harris wasn't worth dying over.

For now, he would stay at Kingfisher and help the sick. Who knows, he may like it so much that he doesn't want to leave. Although, he will need to go to Fort Reno and get medical supplies if he stays much longer. There was enough medication for a while, but it wouldn't last long.

Chapter Thirty

THE FOLLOWING MORNING, BRODY WOKE TO THE sound of rain hitting the roof of his office and thought about sleeping a little longer. The sound of raindrops were pleasing to his ears, but his eyes were wide open, and the room felt a little cold.

Still in nothing but long johns, he made his way into the kitchen and fired up the cookstove. There was another wood stove in the examination room, but he didn't want to go in there until he was dressed. If Emeral happened to be awake, she could see him, and he didn't want that.

With the kitchen heating up, it was time to put on clothes and then check on his patient. If Emeral was still doing better, then he would let her go back to the saloon.

Brody didn't have a full beard, but there was enough hair on his face to make him look rugged and unkept. He still hadn't totally mastered the workings of a straight razor, but the number of nicks to his face was becoming fewer with each time the young man shaved. He liked looking groomed and that included the length of his hair.

Speaking of looking good, Betsy could be by today, and he wanted to impress her with his good looks.

Brody walked to the room where Emeral was, and they talked a few minutes before he pointed to her midsection. "I need to have a look at the stitches and make sure you're still healing correctly."

"You better have your look before your little girlfriend gets here. You know she's jealous that you can see what's under this dress." She busted out laughing at the young, embarrassed man.

The front door opened, and Brody walked that way to find a man soaking wet in the waiting room.

"Is there something I can do for you, mister?"

Water was dripping onto the floor. "You the doctor?"

"Yes, I'm Brody. What do you need?"

"My wife is in a bad way. She's with child and is bleeding something fierce, will you please help her?" the man asked with tears in his eyes.

Brody took a moment to think. "Where do you live?"

"Two miles due south of town, and I know it's raining out there, but we really need you, Doctor. I'll try to pay whatever you want so I don't lose my wife."

"You go to the livery stable and have the hostler saddle my horse while I put together some medication and tools in my bag. Bring the horse here as soon as you can, and I'll be ready."

The man rushed out of the office and Brody started putting different examination tools and medicines in the black doctor bag that belonged to Dr. Stevens. With his hat and slicker on, he stood on the front porch watching for the man to bring his horse to him.

It had already rained so much that morning that the street was mud, and the rain had cut channels down the middle of the road as it made its way to Kingfisher Creek.

As the two men rode south in the driving rain, Brody called out, "What's your name, mister?"

"It's Booker, Booker Purdy, and my wife's name is Susan. I sure hope she's still alive when we get there. This rain has slowed us down."

"Booker, how far along is Susan?"

"You mean how long has she been pregnant?"

"Yes, how many months?"

"I don't rightly know all that, but I reckon about three months, maybe less."

"Has anything like this ever happened to Susan before?"

"Yeah, but not like it is this time. She's miscarried two other times."

Brody put the spurs to the horse and called out, "Come on. Let's take a chance and go faster."

Water and mud were being kicked up into the air by the running horses, and both men's faces were stinging from the rain hitting them in the face. Brody's hat was so wet that the front came down and covered his eyes where he couldn't see. He pushed the hat to the back of his head where it stayed on by the strap.

Two wagons were sitting in front of the house, and the men were met at the door by a short, heavy-set Black man. "She's in bad shape so y'all better come on in here."

———

THREE HOURS later and with the help of two neighbor ladies who are midwives in the community, Susan was finally stable but had miscarried her third baby. Brody paced the floor with Booker sitting on the bed with his wife.

"Listen, this is your third miscarriage, and I'm not sure why it keeps happening, but I highly suggest you don't get pregnant again anytime soon. The next time, it could kill you. I'm sorry, but as a doctor, I have to be honest with you."

Susan wiped tears from her eyes. "But Doctor, we want children so bad."

"I'm sorry, but that's the way it is for now. I'm heading back to town to get some rest. I'll ride out tomorrow to check on you."

Booker got up and walked Brody to the door. "I'm beholden to you, Doctor."

Brody patted Booker on the back and left the house, saddened over the loss of the baby and trouble that the Purdy's wanted children so bad and couldn't have them.

The rain had stopped by the time he rode into Kingfisher, but everything out in the elements were still wet, muddy, and hard to maneuver in. After dropping off his horse, the young man wanted a hot bath and dry clothes, so he headed back to the office where he found Betsy mopping the floors.

"Good morning, beautiful," said Brody when he saw her.

"You got part of the greeting right," said the girl, and dropped the mop and came and kissed him on the lips. "Dr. Brody, it's two in the afternoon."

"In that case, let me wash up and we can go eat dinner, that is unless you want to stay and continue to clean."

She looked at him. "I think you should clean up before you go out."

With a fresh shirt on and his hair combed, the two

made their way to the diner. While eating, Betsy stopped with her fork almost to her mouth. "I almost forgot. Emeral was gone when I got there today. She left you a note on the bed thanking you for saving her life. That poor woman can hardly write, let alone spell some of the words."

"Betsy, Emeral has had a hard life, and it's only going to get harder for her with age. Women in her line of work grow old quick, so give her a break. You or I don't know the circumstances of why she works at the saloon."

Betsy seemed a little shocked by Brody's remarks but smiled and nodded her head. "You're right, and she was nothing more than a patient to you, and I appreciate you taking care of her the way you did." She reached over and put her hand over his and gave it a squeeze.

With his reputation growing each day, Brody took the liberty of walking around town with Betsy, meeting the townsfolk on the street. Going into their homes and sharing a meal, or jawing with them on the boardwalk for a few moments.

The following seven days went by quickly for the young man performing doctor duties of various sicknesses, broken bones, and cuts.

Chapter Thirty-One

A CLOSED FIST POUNDING ON THE FRONT DOOR of the doctor's office woke Brody up from a deep sleep. It took him a few seconds to realize that the noise was coming from the front door. He rolled over in the bed and put his bare feet on the cold floor before easing the pistol out of its holster and laid the gun on the bed while he pulled on his britches.

With the gun in hand, he walked to the door and pulled it open where a young cowboy with blood on his shirt fell into his arms. Brody grabbed the man under his arms and dragged him inside. The man's boot heels dragged against the floor as he was hauled into the examination room. After some straining and using all the strength that he could muster, the doctor was able to get the cowboy on the bed where he could examine where the blood came from.

The man had been stabbed five times and was losing lots of blood. Brody worked fast to put bandages on some of the stab wounds until he could begin sewing the cuts back together. With no one to help him to save the man's life, Brody stayed with the task at hand until he had the bleeding stopped.

The doctor finally stepped back and took a few minutes to get the stove heating so he would have hot water to wash the man's wounds. Brody went into the kitchen and was washing all the blood off his hands, arms, and body. Suddenly, he heard loud talking and knew someone had come in.

Brody grabbed his gun and was in the examination room when three men walked into the room looking for the injured man.

Brody pointed to the door. "You men ain't got no business here. Turn around and leave while you can."

"We've come after this cheating rascal so you might ought to move aside and let us have him," said the man in front with blood on his shirt sleeve.

Brody cocked back the hammer on his pistol. "The last feller that thought he could come in here and take one of my patients is in boot hill. I may not get all three of you, but I can promise you that my first bullet will kill you and then at least one other. So make your move and let's dance."

"I don't think you have the guts to shoot anyone." The man took one step forward before the slug hit him in the chest. His eyes opened wide as he grabbed his chest, and then his knees buckled, causing him to tumble onto the floor face first.

Brody had the gun pointed at the other two men. "Look, I didn't want to have to kill your friend, but he didn't give me much choice. I'm not letting anyone come into my office and take one of my patients without a fight. Now, I suggest you take your dead friend with you and leave here and don't come back."

Still in shock at seeing their friend shot, one man

said, "You didn't have to kill old Lester, but we'll leave you be for now. Come on, Jefferson, let's carry Lester out of here and go have a drink."

Brody watched the two men drag the dead man out of the office and onto the street where they left him and went to the saloon. The doctor didn't trust the two men and put on his boots and shirt before going to the city jail to tell the deputy on duty what happened. The deputy got the undertaker out of bed, and with the help of a couple more men, they were able to load the dead man in the back of a wagon and take him to the undertaker's parlor.

Brody was still up when he heard a noise outside but didn't go out to investigate. He figured it was the two men trying to trick him into coming out. He might be young and inexperienced, but he knew better than to go out where they lay ready to bushwhack him.

The patient started improving, and after four days, Brody let him leave with instructions to come back in a week to have the stitches removed.

Three weeks had passed since Brody sent the letter to his ma, and he was getting antsy to hear back from her. He was also running short of supplies in the doctor's office and made himself a long list of things to buy at Fort Reno.

Brody made arrangements with the owner of the livery stable to rent a pack horse that he could take with him to Fort Reno. The following morning, with the pack horse in tow, the young doctor headed south for the twenty-three-mile trip to the fort.

With not being familiar with where he was going, Brody had the pistol on his right hip and the shoulder holster gun under his left arm. The shoulder holster gun couldn't be seen for the coat the young man wore, and he had a handkerchief tied around his neck to help keep out the cold.

A lot of changes had been made to his appearance since he left Wichita months ago. His hair was short, and the sparse whiskers were shaved off every couple of days. He had changed out his shoes to riding boots and his britches to what cowboys wore on the cattle drives. The one thing that he really liked was the wide-brimmed hat that sat on top of his head. He was now blending in with the locals and if someone saw him they would think he was just another resident.

A small community came into view, and the sign on one of the buildings said, *Okarche*. This would be a nice place to stop for something to eat since he didn't have breakfast before he left Kingfisher. The first diner he saw was where he guided his horses to the hitch rail and dismounted.

Inside the place were a few empty tables where Brody sat down, and when the girl came to take his order, she said, "Hello, mister, you want coffee to drink?"

"No ma'am, I'd like a glass of milk if you have it and eggs and ham."

"Coming right up." The girl headed to the kitchen with his order.

Brody felt a little uneasy for some reason and took the time to look at each person inside the place. The only ones that rustled up his dander were two men sitting to the right of the door, and both men were watching him. That made him uneasy to the point that he reached into his coat and removed the safety from the shoulder holster gun.

About the time that the waitress brought his food to the table, the men got up and left the diner. When Brody finished his meal and pushed the plate out of the way, the waitress came to take the plate, and he asked, "Do you know who those two men were that was sitting by the door?"

"Not really. They been here for a few days looking for someone by the name of Thaddeus. Do you know them?"

"Nope. I ain't never seen them before. Thanks for the food and you have a wonderful day," said Brody, and handed her a dollar.

Before walking outside, he stood to the side of the door where he could see out into the street. The two men were nowhere to be seen, so he went to his horses and mounted up. Only a short distance from the diner was Uncle John's Creek, and that's where the two men sat on their horses waiting on the young man.

Brody knew they were going to question him, and he moved the reins to his left hand and opened the buttons on his coat. Taking his time, he removed the safety off the pistol on his hip and prayed that they wouldn't recognize him.

Still some fifty feet from the men, Brody stopped his horse. "Is there something I can help you fellers with?"

The larger of the two men had the makings in his hand. He went ahead and finished rolling the cigarette before answering. "Thaddeus, it looks like we finally meet up. We been hunting you all over the territory so we can collect our money."

"That's interesting, mister. My name is Dr. Brody Connor, and I'm the only doctor in Kingfisher. I'm sorry that you've mistaken me for whoever this Thaddeus person is. Now, if you would be so kindly to move aside, I'm on my way to Fort Reno to stock up on supplies."

The large man struck a lucifer on the saddle leather and lit the cigarette. The smaller of the two men pointed his finger at Brody. "You ain't going anywhere. Now take off that hat so we can have a good look at you."

"I'll do no such thing. Now move aside so I can be on my way."

The larger man, with the cig dangling between his lips, started his horse forward, and when he did, Brody applied a little pressure to the reins and his horse turned to the left. Brody reached inside his coat and pulled out his gun.

With the gun pointed at the man who was within ten feet of him, he asked, "Mister, are you going to die over mistaken identity?"

The large man stopped, took a puff off the cig, and blew out the smoke. "Horace said you was a dangerous little cuss. He said you killed his brother in cold blood. Well, you may get off one shot but that's not going to keep us from killing you and collecting the two hundred that Horace is going to pay us."

The man flipped the cigarette to the ground, dropped his hand to his gun handle and that's when two bullets hit him in the chest. Brody didn't wait to see the results, he turned the gun to the other man and fired as the man took aim.

The first man he shot was lying on the ground, and the second man was wounded but still alive when Brody took him off the horse and looked at where he was hit. The bullet had hit him in the chest, and the blood that was flowing out looked like it was coming from his liver by the color.

"You men had a chance to step aside but chose not to. Who's Horace, and why was he paying you to kill Thaddeus?"

"He's the boy's uncle. He hired us to kill the boy so he could take over the tavern."

"That didn't work out for you, did it? So the law didn't send you to find Thaddeus?"

"No, the law didn't care about the boy."

The man died within seconds and that's where Brody left the two men and mounted up. He wouldn't have to keep watch on his back trail anymore now that the two men were dead. It saddened him a little that he had to take two lives, but they had every opportunity to let him pass.

Chapter Thirty-Two

BRODY RODE THROUGH WHAT HE THOUGHT WAS a town but soon realized it was the Darlington Indian Agency on the north bank of the North Canadian River. On the south bank of the river was the sprawling Fort Reno, comprised of many barracks and officer housing.

The Darlington Indian Agency was also much more than he had expected as he rode through on his way to cross the North Canadian River. There was a large school for the Cheyenne and Arapaho Indian children. Close by was a store where the reservation Indians could get food, clothing, cooking utensils, and anything else they needed. The agency's hospital was so busy that Indians were sitting outside waiting to see a doctor. Closer to the river were pens full of cattle and horses. The odd thing to Brody was the location of the agency. It was located along the North Canadian River where it intersected with the Chisholm Trail. Every herd of cattle coming up the Chisholm Trail went past the reservation.

The agency and the surrounding area was clean, and the facilities were well-kept. As Brody rode through, many of the natives watched but none made any motions to wave or acknowledge his presence.

Crossing the North Canadian River wasn't a problem with the shallow water and red sand that covered the ground. Fort Reno was huge compared to the few army forts that the young man had been on in the past. There were all sorts and sizes of buildings and businesses to support the soldiers stationed at the fort.

What he didn't know was the fact that the 10th Cavalry was stationed at the fort and the 10th were all Black soldiers. Along the river were numerous pens of horses and cattle to support the troops with transportation and food.

Brody stopped a soldier as he crossed in front of him. "Where will I find the post doctor?"

The man pointed to the south. "The infirmity is down that way. It's a big building made out of rock."

The soldier was right. The building served as the post hospital as well as where the doctors worked. Brody went inside and introduced himself to the soldier sitting at a table. "I'm Dr. Brody Connor from Kingfisher, and I'm here to get medical supplies if I can."

"I'll let the captain know you're here. You can have a seat over there," said the soldier, pointing to chairs.

Brody took the seat, and in less than ten minutes, the army officer came out in a white apron covering the front of his uniform with splotches of blood on it.

"I'm Dr. Duval, and who might you be?"

Brody stood up and extended his hand. "I'm Dr. Brody Connor from Kingfisher. I took over Dr. Stevens's office, and I'm running low on supplies and was hoping that I could purchase some from the army."

"We're not in the habit of selling supplies. You can go to the Sutlers Store and buy what's there." He turned to the private sitting at the desk. "Private, escort our guest to the Sutlers Store and tell them to sell him what he needs."

He turned back to Brody. "You can also stop at the store across the river on the reservation if you're willing to treat the Indians. The hospital has a wide range of supplies but are short on doctors. You may be able to strike a deal where you can get supplies if you're willing to treat some of the sick Indians at your office."

"Thanks for all your help, Captain."

"Sorry, I couldn't do more. I have to go now."

Brody followed the private to the store where he was only able to get some of the things he needed. Alcohol, bandages, and carbolic acid were all the store had. Brody packed those items away and headed toward the Indian Agency hospital.

He met an old army doctor at the hospital by the name of Mathews. After explaining his situation, Brody was taken to the Indian Agent whose name was John Homer Seger. Brody made a deal with Seger that he would treat Indians off the reservation which was only a mile west of Kingfisher in exchange for medical tools and supplies.

When Brody had packed all his newly acquired supplies on the packhorse and was riding north, he spotted a post office in the agency compound. Out of curiosity, he stopped at the post office and went inside and asked the postmaster if there was any mail for Brody Connor.

"No, but I do remember a letter with that name on it. I believe it was delivered up the line to Kingfisher."

"Thanks."

Brody had intended to spend the night on the trail, but with the information about his letter being back in town, the young man decided to ride back to Kingfisher that night.

It was dark by the time he made it to Okarche and getting colder. His horses were tired and so was he. There was no way to get the letter from his ma tonight. So he stopped at the livery stable, left the horses, and went to the town's only hotel to get checked in. He then went to the only café that was also a saloon for supper.

Brody sat eating his meal when two men walked in, and one of them stood in front of his table while the other man stood to his left.

"Are you that doctor from Kingfisher?"

Brody put down his fork and put his hand inside his coat where he took off the safety on the shoulder holster gun. "Yes, I'm Dr. Brody. What can I do for you?"

"You killed a friend of ours by the name of Harris."

"Yep, I did kill Harris. He almost beat a girl to death and was on his way to finish her off when I stopped him. Was he such a good friend that you're willing to die over him?"

"What does that mean?" asked the man with a confused look on his face.

"I'm thinking you men are wanting to get revenge for me killing Harris, and I was wondering if a dead man is worth dying for." That's when Brody started biting his bottom lip.

The men looked at each other and then the man smiled at Brody. "Harris was mean to women, and if that's the way it was going down when you killed him, I reckon he had it coming. Sorry to disturb your supper. But I do have one question. Harris was fast with that pistol. Did you face him straight up, or was the fight a different way?"

165

"I faced him straight up, and he wasn't fast enough." Brody picked up his fork and started to eat again.

"Nice meeting you, Dr. Brody. My name is Edmond and he's Mitch. You may not know this but killing Harris has given you the reputation of being a fast gun."

Brody thought about that for a moment before replying. "I'm not sure that's how I want to be known. I hope the reputation would be one that said that I helped sick people. Some might even call me a healer."

"Enjoy your supper, we'll be seeing you," said Edmond, and the two men left.

Chapter Thirty-Three

BRODY WASN'T READY FOR BED JUST YET AND decided to walk to the saloon where he could watch men play poker and try to learn from them. He had played with Emeral and knew what the order of cards were, but he wasn't ready to play for money. After thirty minutes of watching, he grew bored and walked to the hotel.

His room wasn't much, but it did have a soft bed, and as he was getting ready to lay down, there were gunshots down the street. This wasn't his town, and not knowing anyone, he went to the window to see what the commotion was all about.

The batwing doors on the saloon were being held open by a man and then another man came running and stumbling out the door with blood on the front of his shirt. More shots could be heard from inside the saloon and then the man running from the place fell face first into the street.

The shooter came out of the building and fired one more shot into the man on the ground and then he spit on the dead man before he went to his horse and mounted up.

As he was turning his horse to leave, two more men came out and mounted up and went with the first man.

Brody buckled on his guns, grabbed his coat, and rushed out of the hotel. Men were checking on the guy who had been shot, and the constable was also there when Brody showed up. "Let me in here. I'm a doctor."

The men moved aside and one of them said, "You're too late. He's already dead. I reckon he got caught cheating at cards one too many times."

The man was indeed dead, and as Brody was standing back up, one of the bystanders leaned over and pulled the ace of spades from the man's shirt sleeve. "I reckon he used this ace one too many times." The man flipped the card and it landed on the corpse's bloody shirt.

Brody walked back to the hotel and it took him a little while to get the image of the man lying in the dirt street out of his mind. Was it really worth dying to make a few dollars cheating at cards? Then he thought about his situation and tears welled up in his eyes. He had killed Ludwig. He wanted to think it was an accident when he tripped on the leg of the chair, but he had went there that day to kill the man. The men looking for him were also dead, and he hoped there wasn't more on his backtrail.

This journey he was on has been one of learning to survive on his own with the help of some fine people. Thinking of that, he had to wonder if the Mosleys had made it to their so-called promise land. Bob wasn't a fighter, and if it wasn't for his son, Lester, they may not make it.

Then he thought about William, the old Indian who had taught him so much about fighting, drawing a gun, and of course, the main thing was the plants that produced healing medicine to treat different ailments. He hoped to stop by and see William on his way back to Kansas, that is, if he ever gets to go back.

―――――

THE FOLLOWING MORNING, Brody was heading north after a big breakfast. The morning was cold, and his horses were more than ready to travel a little faster to warm their bodies.

The doctor's office was the first stop when he arrived in Kingfisher so he could unload all the medical supplies. He could tell that someone had been in the reception room by one of the chairs being out of place. With the safety off his gun, the young man walked into each room to make sure he didn't have someone inside waiting to harm him.

While in the kitchen, he went ahead and lit a fire in the cookstove and one in the potbelly stove in the examining room. The air outside was getting colder, and a hint of moisture was in the atmosphere.

It would take a while to get the office warm, and he took that time to unload and then take the horses to the livery stable. On his way back, he stopped at the post office and asked Lucille, the postmaster, if he had a letter.

She handed him the letter. "Is this from your mother?"

"I sure hope so. Thanks, Lucille."

Brody wanted to tear open the envelope but restrained himself until he was back inside where it was getting warm. He went into the kitchen and sat down before opening the letter.

Dear Thaddeus,

It's so good to finally hear from you. The law is not looking for you. The men in the tavern testified that you tripped and the gun went off by accident. I've missed you so much since you've been gone, but I'm also afraid of Ludwig's brother. He is a mean man and took the tavern away from me. Now I have to work for him. You have to be careful, he sent two men to kill you, and I'm scared for your life. Dr. Melrose came by to let me know that you were accepted into the doctor school in Kansas City. I hope you get this letter and go there so you can make something of your life.

I love you.

Brody read the letter three times before he leaned back and thought about his future. What was he going to do? The law wasn't after him, but there was Ludwig's brother to contend with. The man seemed to be as mean as Ludwig was, and he didn't like the fact that the man took the tavern away from his mother.

There was also Betsy, the girl he really liked and thought a lot of. Could he leave her to go back to Wichita to take care of business? Then there was medical school. His mother said that he had been accepted there, and that was his dream.

These last few months since he left home had broadened his knowledge about helping people. He had studied books, but most importantly, he had actually administered medical services on real people that had real ailments.

What about Kingfisher and the surrounding area? If he left now, they would be without any doctors in the area. He had met some mighty fine folks here who had welcomed him with open arms.

The door to the reception office opened, and Brody headed that way to see who had come in. It was Emeral and another of the saloon girls that he had never met before.

"Hi Emeral, is everything okay?"

"Yes, Brody, I'm fine. This is Lilly, and she has a big problem that needs your assistance."

"Hi Lilly, come on in and tell me what's going on with you."

"Well, doctor, it's like this. I'm pregnant and I need to get rid of the baby."

Brody was a little shaken by the request and this was a new one for him, and he didn't have an answer for her for a few moments. He walked over to his cabinet and retrieved the only stethoscope in the office.

"Lilly, let's get you on the examining table so I can check you out."

He took hold of her arm and assisted her onto the table.

"Why do you think that you're with child?"

"I've been missing my time of the month, and I'm throwing up every morning. My stomach is growing, and I can't take care of a brat kid in my line of work."

"I see," said Brody, and put the stethoscope to the woman's stomach and started to move it around. When he finished, he helped her sit up and then put the tool away before he came back and sat in one of the chairs.

"Listen, I'm no expert on childbirth or about unborn babies, but I know a heartbeat when I hear it. That baby is a living person with a heartbeat, and I will not kill it. I'm sorry, but this is not something that I can do."

"But I can't take care of a kid at the saloon. Please, doctor, push something up there and make it come out," pleaded the woman.

Brody suddenly stood up. "Will you listen to another option that I just thought of?"

Chapter Thirty-Four

ANOTHER OPTION, WHAT DO YOU MEAN?" ASKED Lilly.

"I know a couple that can't have a baby of their own, and I was wondering if I can work out a deal with them, then you could go live with them, and when the baby comes, they can raise it, and you can go back to work. Is that something you would be open to do?"

Emeral came to Lilly and took her hands in hers. "Lilly, think about what the doctor is offering you. This could help you out, and that couple can give your baby a good home."

Lilly didn't say anything for a few seconds. "This is a lot to think about. I need to have some time to digest all this, and I should talk to my boss and see if I can go back to work after the baby is born."

Brody reached down and patted her on the back. "That's all I ask. You're at least three months pregnant and I really think more than that. If you decide to take me up on the offer, then I'll go talk to the couple."

After the two women left, Brody sat and thought

about Lilly's situation. He had stuck to his moral convictions and refused to kill the unborn child. Lilly was a saloon girl and didn't know who the father was. The offer for her to live with Booker and Susan Purdy seemed like a win all the way around. Now he would wait and see what Lilly decided.

The rest of the day, Brody put up the supplies he purchased and treated a few patients for minor illness. Betsy came to see him that afternoon and he sat her down so he could talk. "I've heard from my ma, and she said I had been accepted to the new medical school in Kansas City. I want you to know that I'm thinking about leaving and becoming the best doctor I can be. I really care for you and that's the only reason I haven't already left."

Betsy smiled at her boyfriend and then took his hands into his. "Brody, I knew that you would leave someday. I want you to go to medical school and become a great doctor. You have all the qualities for it, and the thing I love most about you is that you don't compromise your patients when the going gets rough. I could never live with myself if I thought that I was holding you back, so when you're ready to leave, I'll be the first to see you off."

Brody wiped tears from his eyes. This was the nicest thing someone had ever said to him, and he put his arms around Betsy and kissed her.

When they broke their embraces, she asked, "When are you planning on leaving?"

"I'm not sure. I have something important concerning one of the saloon girls that I want to see through."

"Are you talking about Lilly?"

"Yes. What do you know about her?"

"I know she's pregnant and wants someone to kill her baby. Are you thinking about doing that?"

"No, I won't do that. I may take a life but it's in self-defense or I'm protecting one of my patients. I've given her another option, and I hope she takes it."

"I knew you wouldn't do it. You're a good man, Brody Connor."

"Do you know Booker and Susan Purdy? They can't have children, and I want Lilly to go and live with them until the baby is born. They will make great parents to her baby."

Betsy smiled. "That's a wonderful idea, I'm going to go talk to Lilly right now and tell her what I think about that idea." Betsy leaned over and kissed Brody and took off.

Not long after Betsy left, two riders pulled up to the hitching rail out front, and Brody watched as one of the men dismounted and went to help the second man get off his horse. The second man's thigh was bloody, and his pants had a large rip in it.

Brody met them at the door. "Take him in that room and let's get him on the bed so I can examine that thigh."

It took Brody and the other cowboy to get the injured man on the bed. As Brody went after a pair of scissors, he asked, "What happened to him?"

"He took a horn to his thigh. It went in pretty far."

"I'm going to cut your britches so I can see how bad the wound is."

"Mister, these are the only britches that I own and if it's okay with you, I'd rather take them off."

"That's fine. What's your name?"

"It's Rufus, the ugly one over there is my foreman, and his name is Delmer."

175

Delmer went to the foot of the bed. "Let me help you get your boots off."

When the boots were off, Brody helped Rufus out of his britches. The wound was still bleeding, and the hole was ragged and infected. Brody washed the wound with bromide and then iodine, which caused the cowboy to raise up on the bed from the sting and burning of the medicine.

"I'm going to make a paste out of some Indian herbs and plants to stop the bleeding. The wound is so deep and big around that I need it to start to heal some before I stitch it up. If I can find something to put in the hole so it will drain, then I can go ahead and sew it up."

Delmer took off his hat, and his bald head was covered in sweat. "Doctor, I have a herd of cattle ten miles south of here heading to Wichita, Kansas. I need this man in the saddle as soon as possible."

"Leave him here for the night, and I'll try to get him up and ready as soon as I can, but there's no guarantees that he can ride."

Delmer left, and Brody looked in all the cabinets but couldn't find anything he could use as a drain. He walked to the hardware store and bought a short length of copper tubing that he could sterilize and sew into the wound to drain the liquid so it would heal from the inside.

He used chloroform to put Rufas out long enough to sew the hole up with the copper tube in it. He could always remove the tube when the healing started.

———

THAT NIGHT while lying in bed, a new thought came to him. Delmer had said he had a herd of cattle on the way to Wichita, and Brody thought that if he could join up with the herd, then he could take his meals there and he could learn how to herd cattle. That was something he had wanted to do when he was younger, and this was the ideal time to learn. If Delmer would let him help with the cattle then Rufus could ride in the chuckwagon and let his leg heal. That way, Delmer didn't lose a hand, and Rufus could use the time to get back to normal.

Someone was rasping on the front door, and Brody got out of bed, grabbed one of his guns, and made his way to the door. Lilly was there with a man that Brody had seen around town.

"Come on in," said Brody, and moved to the side of the door.

"I'm sorry to bother you, Doctor, but I wanted to talk to you some more. This is my boss, Jerome Festus, from the saloon and he also has some questions."

"I'm glad you're back and it's nice to meet you, Jerome," said Brody, and stuck out his hand.

"I've seen you around town and I've heard some good things about you, Doctor. I really appreciate what you did for Emeral. I was wondering if Lilly decides to give up her child, when would she have to go live with the folks? I'm already shorthanded at the saloon and was thinking that if I could have Lilly deal cards at one of the tables or work in the café, she could continue to work until she was closer to having the baby."

"I don't see an issue with Lilly continuing to work as long as she thinks she's able. I'm thinking that for the last month she should be with the folks and probably stay with them a couple of days until she is well enough to come back to town. Lilly, are you leaning toward letting those folks raise your baby as theirs?"

"Yes, I am, and I think this conversation has made up

my mind. If you want to talk to the people tomorrow and make sure they're willing, then I'll go along with it."

Brody was smiling. "That's great news. The people that I'm going to talk to are Booker and Susan Purdy. They've tried multiple times to have a child and it's to the point that it could put her life in danger. Do either of you know them?"

"Yes, I know both of them, and I couldn't ask for a nicer couple to have my baby."

"Well, it seems that we have a deal," said Jerome. "Come on Lilly, let's go back to the saloon."

"I'll be talking to you tomorrow," said Brody, and they left.

Chapter Thirty-Five

BRODY WAS ON THE ROAD TO THE PURDY'S FARM shortly after daylight. He wanted to get this situation settled so he could start planning on leaving Kingfisher for Kansas.

Smoke was coming out of the chimney, and he could see Booker outside gathering firewood in his arms when he rode into the yard.

"Morning, Doctor, come on in, the coffee's hot." Booker took the double arm load into the house with Brody following along. They went into the kitchen where Susan was cooking breakfast.

Susan pointed the fork she was using at the table. "Have a seat Brody, and I'll get you a cup of coffee. I'm fixing breakfast and have plenty if you ain't eaten yet."

Brody sat down. "I would appreciate the breakfast, but I don't drink coffee. I never acquired a taste for it,"

"I hear that," said Susan. "I have to doctor it up with sugar and cream."

They made small talk while Susan cooked. He asked how she was doing physically since he was there a few days ago. When everyone finished eating, Brody scooted back from the table. "I have an important proposition for the two of you. I have a patient that is with child and wants to know if the two of you will take it when it's born and raise it as your own."

Susan broke down and started to cry. "You darn right we'll take that baby. Oh, thank you so much Lord, and you too, Doctor."

Booker looked at his wife and then at Brody. "You tell that woman that she's welcome to come live with us, and we'll take care of her. She can stay as long as she wants."

Brody continued. "I'll be honest with you. It's Lilly from the saloon, and she's most likely three or four months pregnant. She's made arrangements with her boss to continue working until the time is closer, and then she'll come live with you. I know the two of you will be great parents to that child."

Susan wiped off the tears. "I'm so excited. You tell Lilly that she is welcome here anytime."

Brody got up and stuck out his hand to shake. Susan got up and put her arms around the young doctor. "Thank you, Brody. We were about to give up on ever getting a child."

Brody patted her on the back. "They say the Lord works in mysterious ways, and I reckon he does. I'm really happy for the two of you."

She turned him loose, and Booker shook his hand. When they were finished, Brody started for the door. "I'm going back to town and will tell Lilly the good news. I'm leaving Kingfisher to go to medical school in Kansas City, so you may not see me much after today, but I'll have it all worked out before I leave town. I understand that you know Betsy. She may be the go-between you all and Lilly. I'll be in touch."

Brody headed back to town but stopped by to tell Betsy the whole story and see if she would be the person to take his place in the matter of the baby.

She agreed, and his next stop was the saloon where Lilly greeted him when he came in. "Have you seen the Purdy's yet?" she asked.

"Yes, and they're so excited. They said to tell you that you're welcome to come live with them whenever you're ready to, and you can stay as long as you desire. I've also talked to Betsy, and she's taking my place with this, so you can tell her whatever you want. I'm going back to Kansas to enroll into medical school and will be leaving soon."

Lilly put her hand to her mouth. "Oh my, you won't be here to deliver my baby."

"No, I probably won't be. I'm still hoping that Dr. Stevens comes back soon. But don't you fret none about the baby. I'm sure there are midwives here with more experience in childbirth than I have."

He left the saloon and went back to the office to find three people already in the waiting area. The patients finally slacked off after dinner time, and Brody was able to change out the dressing on Rufus's thigh. The wound was red and inflamed with some seepage. Brody cleaned it with carbolic acid and put on a clean dressing.

That afternoon he found himself treating more patients until it was almost dark. When Brody was having his supper he saw Delmer and four cowboys ride into town. Delmer broke off from his men and headed toward the office. Brody got up, went to the door, and whistled. Delmer saw him and turned toward the café which was beside the saloon.

Brody pointed to the table. "Pull up a chair and have some supper."

"I'll have coffee. I ate with the men at the cow camp before we came to town."

Brody pushed his plate over. "I may have come up with a solution to you not being able to use Rufus for a while. I need to go back to Wichita, and I can take his place with the cattle drive, and Rufus can ride in the wagon. That way, I can keep watch on his wound and take up the slack driving the cattle."

Delmer poured coffee out of the cup onto the saucer. He picked it up with both hands and slurped the hot liquid down. "Do you know anything about cattle or how to work cattle out on the trail?"

"No, I don't, but I'm a fast learner and will work hard. I just don't want to make the trip back to Kansas by myself."

"Look, you're a greenhorn and the men will have a heyday with you out there. They'll ride you hard and may even try to rough you up some. I'm not sure you're up to the challenge of going on a cattle drive," said Delmer. "We're still between twelve and fifteen days out of Wichita, and those men can be a mite mean to a new hand that don't know diddily squat about cows."

Brody never flinched. "I can take care of myself with those men as long as they don't all come at me at the same time. One-on-one and I'll be the winner every time with fist or guns."

Delmer stood up. "Thanks for the coffee. I'm going to go check on Rufus and then have a few drinks at the saloon. I'll be thinking about your suggestion."

Chapter Thirty-Six

DELMER LEFT, AND BRODY SAT THINKING ABOUT what the man said. He would have to prove himself to the cowhands and it could be a fight every day. William had taught him well, and if it was a fair one-on-one he would welcome the activity.

Not being one to shy away from a fight, he decided to walk to the saloon and wait until Delmer returned before he took the fight to the men he saw come in with the foreman.

The cowhands were all sitting together at one of the tables where a half-empty whiskey bottle sat in the middle of the table. Each man had a glass in front of them and were talking to the working girls as they came by.

Brody stayed away from their table until Delmer came in and sat down. Brody walked over to the table and took a chair from another table and sat with the four cow punchers.

Brody sat where he could get up quickly. "Delmer, are you going to introduce me to the hands?"

The cowhands were all taken back with the young man's aggression. Delmer looked at Brody and shook his head back and forth. "Boy, you're sure looking to get whipped like a red-headed stepchild, ain't you?"

Brody grinned and came around with a haymaker and hit the man to his right, knocking him out of his chair. He then stood up and hit the man on his left square on the chin and knocked him out.

Delmer sat watching the fight as the third man took off around the table toward Brody, who dropped down on one knee and used his other leg to sweep the man's legs out from under him. The man fell on his back and was getting up when Brody hit him with a right, a left, and another right that landed on the cowboy's temple, knocking him unconscious.

The man he hit first was getting up when Brody kicked him on the back of his knee with just the right amount of force to take the man to his knees. Brody grabbed a hand full of the drover's hair and looked at Delmer. "What's it going to be? Do I continue on, or will you give me the job?"

Delmer threw back the shot of whiskey. "It looks like you have the job. We leave in the morning right after daylight. I'll have the chuckwagon come pick up Rufus and you can join up then. Be sure and bring your coat and bedroll."

Brody frowned. "I'm not sure that tomorrow morning is giving us enough time with Rufus. If his wound gets infected or starts bleeding on the trail, he could be in real danger."

Delmer refilled his glass. "I have a herd that has to be delivered in Wichita as soon as we can get them there. I can't afford to wait around on Rufus to heal up."

The men that Brody whipped were coming to, and

by the look on their faces, they were still somewhat in awe that the young man had knocked the three of them out.

Delmer took the bottle and filled the glasses before talking to his men. "You men take a seat, and I'll introduce you to the new hand that's taking Rufus's place until he's able to work again."

Brody stood up and extended his hand to the first man to get seated. "I'm Brody Connor and it's going to be fun getting to know you all."

"I'm Mitchel, and you got a might strong right fist for a greenhorn."

The next man was named Chester, who was still rubbing his chin where Brody had hit him.

After he had shaken the hands of all three of the men, the last feller held on to his hand. "I'm Winfred and it ain't over between the two of us. The next time we tangle it'll be a fair fight."

"Good, I'm looking forward to knocking you out again," said Brody, never breaking a smile. He then turned back to Delmer. "I have an idea if you're willing to listen."

"I'll listen."

"You can leave Rufus at Dr. Stevens's office, and I can make arrangements for someone to clean Rufus's wound and put on clean dressings each day. They'll also make sure he has food to eat and anything else that he needs. Someone will have to pay the person that's going to see after him.".

Delmer held up a finger. "Hold on a second. If I leave Rufus here, then you can ride with us tomorrow, and someone will see after Rufus until he can manage on his own."

"That's right. I can leave here in the morning and that

way we don't have to doctor Rufus on the trail, and you can pick him up on your way back home."

Delmer looked at the others. "What do you men think of Brody's idea?"

Winfred drank down the remaining whiskey in his glass and looked at Brody. "As much as I want to beat on this greenhorn whipper snapper, I think it's a grand idea. This way Rufus will be taken care of and we won't be totally shorthanded."

The other two men were nodding their heads in acknowledgment, and Chester poured whiskey into a glass and pushed it over to Brody. "Let's see if you're man enough to have a drink with us and seal the deal."

Brody knew the man had him at a disadvantage and thought he would choke on the stout alcohol. What Chester didn't know was the fact that Brody had taken a few drinks of whiskey before and knew how. He picked up the glass and as he was putting it to his lips, he blew out the air in his lungs and swallowed the shot in one gulp. He never blinked or made a face as the liquor burned all the way down to his stomach. He turned the glass over and set it on the top of the table.

"I reckon that seals the deal, and I'll see you at daylight in the morning. I have a lot to do by the morning, so I'll make my exit."

Chapter Thirty-Seven

BETSY WAS FIRST ON HIS LIST OF THINGS TO DO and that's where the young man headed when he left the saloon. Betsy came to the door and invited him in when he had lightly tapped on the door frame. She kissed him on the lips and jerked her head back. "You've been drinking whiskey, Brody Connor."

"Let me explain. I made a deal to go with the herd that Rufus works with and I had to take one drink to seal the deal."

She kissed him again. "Well! You're a grown man and can have a drink if you want to."

"I'm not one to drink as you well know. I made a deal where Rufus could stay at the office and heal, but I need you to look after him, and you may have to clean his wound and put a fresh bandage on it. You'll also have to make sure he has food until he's able to fend for himself."

She took a few seconds to think about his request and then said, "I'll do it for you. But you have to promise to write me when you get to medical school."

Brody smiled and put his arms around her. "I promise to write you every chance I get." Then he kissed her. They spent the next thirty minutes talking, and as he was getting ready to leave, she grabbed her coat and went with him.

Brody showed her how to clean Rufus's wound and where the supplies were to treat him. After she left to go back home, Brody packed his bedroll and an extra change of clothing and made sure that he had his rain slicker and plenty of bullets for his gun.

It wasn't dark yet, and he heard horses running outside, and when he looked out the window, five cowboys were dismounting in front of the saloon. He had never seen these men before and wondered if another herd was coming through or was it local men who worked on a ranch.

It was none of his business and he went into the kitchen to cook himself and Rufus supper of ham and eggs. When the meal was finished and he had cleaned up his mess, three shots rang out from across the street somewhere.

Brody grabbed his hat and coat off the wall and went to the front door. Delmer and his men were standing in the street, and Mitchel had blood on the side of his face. The five men that Brody had seen minutes ago were standing on the boardwalk with their guns drawn on Delmer and his men.

Brody walked straight across the street and down the boardwalk until he was within five feet of the man doing all the talking.

"I told you last year that if I ever seen any of your bunch again that I would kill the lot of you," screamed the man to Delmer.

Delmer tried to ease the tension. "Now, Hubert, that ain't no way to talk to me. I told you a year ago that I was sorry about your brother getting trampled by those cattle. It was all his fault, and he shouldn't have tried to turn those stampeding longhorns."

"I'm going to kill all of you and take your cattle as payment for my brother," said Hubert.

Brody made his move and took two steps toward Hubert, and when he did, he put the barrel of his gun against the side of the man's head. "I do believe that you will die here today, Mr. Hubert. Now either make your play or lower that pistol. It's all up to you now."

Hubert stayed focused on Delmer. "I don't think you have the guts to shoot me, boy."

Brody had to think quick. "Well, Harris Chumbley didn't think that either and he's six feet under now, so what's it going to be?"

Hubert lowered his gun and put it in its holster, then pointed a finger at Delmer. "This ain't over, and I intend to kill you the first chance I get."

Brody took a few steps backward and put his gun in its holster. "Hubert, I work for Delmer and if you really want to kill someone, then I suggest you turn toward me and pull leather. I ride for Delmer, and a fight with him is a fight with me."

Hubert began to sweat profusely and then raised his hands to chest level. "I ain't no gun fighter and I ain't drawing against you. Come on boys, lets head back to the herd." And he started off the steps leading to the street.

"Hold on," said Brody. "I'm not going to look over my shoulder all the way to Wichita. If I suspect that you or any of your men are going to cause us harm out on the trail, then I'm coming for you, and I won't give you a second chance again. Is that understood?"

"You have my word that we won't cause any trouble on the trail." Hubert walked to his horse, and he and his men mounted up and rode out of town.

Delmer walked to where Brody stood. "Thanks, Brody. That was a close one, and I appreciate you stepping in.

"Yeah, well, he's a big blowhard. When the tables were turned, he tucked tail and ran. I suggest you have someone watch your back trail tonight, and I'll see you in the morning."

Brody noticed a well-dressed man on a horse pull up in front of the office and go inside. Crossing the street, thinking it was someone that needed help, Brody went inside to find the man in the room with Rufus.

"Is there something I can help you with, mister?"

"I'm Dr. Stevens, and I'm wanting to know what you men are doing in my office."

Brody stuck out his hand. "I'm Brody Connor, and I've been using your office to treat sick and injured townsfolk. I'm sure glad to see you back Dr. Stevens."

"Who gave you permission to take over my office, young man?"

"Well, sir, the mayor said I could use it since you up and left. But you don't have to fret none. I restocked all your supplies and even added a few things. In the morning, I'm leaving here and heading to Kansas City to enroll in the new medical school there."

"I see," said the doctor. "I take it that you're not a doctor but someone that is pretending to be one."

"Not really, I worked with Dr. Melrose in Wichita for two years and I've spent time with an Indian medicine man. I've also studied three medical books that I own and the ones you have. I've never said I was a doctor, but when someone is hurting, I'll help them if I can."

The doctor walked into the kitchen and then came back to the room where Rufus was. "I would appreciate it if you would take your things and leave my office. The injured man can stay, but it's time for you to leave."

"Sure thing, but I need to tell you a few things first. Susan Purdy had another miscarriage, and I told them to stop trying to have a baby. Lilly, one of the saloon girls is pregnant, and I've made a deal with her and the Purdy's for her to live with them when it gets closer for the child to be born. The Purdy's will raise the child as their own. I would appreciate it if you would watch over Lilly."

Dr. Stevens's sour expression changed and he smiled. "Maybe you ain't so bad after all. I'll keep watch on Lilly and the man in the bed in there. It looks like he's got a nasty hole in his thigh."

"He got gored by a longhorn, and I sewed a tube in the wound so the infection would drain out. He still has a little infection, but it's healing from the inside out. I have plenty of carbolic acid, bromide, and iodine to fight the infection. That cabinet over there is full of sterilized bandages. I'll take my things and be on my way. I'm riding with a herd of drovers to Wichita and I might as well go on out there tonight."

"You can stay here one more night if you want."

"No thanks, I might as well start learning to sleep out on the ground. It's still a few days before we make it to Wichita. I made arrangements for Betsy to come by and take care of Rufus and to make sure he has food to eat. I would appreciate it if you would tell her that she doesn't have to do that."

"I know Betsy, and I'll take care of your request." The doctor stuck out his hand. "I wish you well in your schooling, Brody."

"Thanks, Doctor." Brody took his things outside and walked toward the livery stable.

Chapter Thirty-Eight

BRODY DROPPED HIS POSSESSIONS OFF AT THE livery and started walking toward Betsy's house. Since he was leaving tonight, he wanted to see her again and hoped she wasn't mad at him for taking off.

As he turned onto the street where the girl lived, a shot rang out and he heard the whine of the bullet as it went past his head. This was no time to dilly-dally around, and he hit the ground and rolled where he lay on the ground four feet from a tree. He couldn't see anyone in the darkness, and whoever had fired the shot at him was most likely still out there.

Where he was lying, someone could see his dark form on the ground. Brody crawled until he was able to hide behind the tree and that's when he saw someone running from a tree to a bush. He raised his gun to shoot but then remembered what William Longtooth had taught him. Never be the first one to shoot in the dark, and when someone fires his gun at you, shoot at the fire coming out of the other person's muzzle.

Brody eased himself to his feet behind the tree and

waited. Every once in a while he thought he saw movement but had to be sure before he fired. The night was quiet, and all he could hear was the sound of crickets rubbing their wings together.

He needed some way to draw out his assailant, so he leaned down to find a stick to put his hat on. He began to wave the hat around with his left hand while ready to shoot with his right hand. Shortly after he started using his hat, he saw the fire from the barrel of a gun and fired two quick shots in the location where the shot came from. Three more shots were fired at him, and he heard the bullets hit the tree he was behind.

Brody returned fire and heard someone yell out in pain. He waited and then saw someone running toward the location he had shot at. Taking careful aim, he fired one time, and the man went down at the edge of the street.

Now it was a waiting game to see if any more shots were fired at him. The wait was short-lived when people in houses started to light lanterns, and one man even came outside with a shotgun. "Who's out here shooting up the place?" he asked.

Brody kept quiet and waited. He knew that at least two men were hurt but there could be more waiting on him. Some folks with lanterns could be seen coming from off of Main Street, and Brody waited until he knew who they were.

It looked to be the town marshal and four other men, all armed, and they spread out as they started down the street that the shooting was on.

One of the men called out, "Marshal, there's a dead man over here."

"You men keep your distance and keep looking for more," said the marshal.

Brody called out, "Marshal, it's me, Brody. I'm over here behind this tree. I think there are at least three men hurt out there. They tried to bushwhack me, and I defended myself."

"Brody, show yourself."

"No, sir, there could still be another one hiding to put a bullet in me."

"I'm coming over to you, so don't shoot," said the lawman.

"Who are those men?" asked the marshal.

"I'm not sure. I haven't taken a look at them. I was walking to see Betsy when someone shot at me. The bullet was so close that I could hear it go by. I fell to the ground and hid behind this tree."

"How did you shoot those men over there?"

"I shot at the fire on the end of their gun barrels. I reckon I got lucky."

The marshal turned to where his men were searching and asked, "Have you found any more men out there hiding?"

"No, sir, Marshal. We ain't found no one but these three cowboys from the cattle drive that came into town today."

Brody stepped away from the tree. "Let's go have a look at those men."

The men held the lanterns so Brody and the marshal could get a good look at the cowhands. They were three of the fellers that were with Hubert earlier today.

After Brody looked at each man, he addressed the marshal. "I saw these men with a drover by the name of Hubert. He was going to kill Delmer, another drover, over something that happened to his brother. I stopped him from shooting Delmer, so I reckon he had it in for me."

"I know who Hubert is. He causes trouble every time he comes to town. You watch your back trail with that one. I don't put it past him to try you again," said the marshal.

"Yeah, I certainly will." Brody commenced to reload his gun. "I'm going to go see Betsy now if that's all right with you, Marshal."

"I'm about finished here. You go on about your business."

Brody walked on to Betsy's house, and they were able to sit on the porch swing for one last time. He didn't tell her anything about the shooting but did tell her that Dr. Stevens was back and she didn't have to check on Rufus after all.

After some kisses, crying and hugs, Brody walked away, saddened that he may never see the sweet girl again. He turned his attention away from Betsy and back on the fact that Hubert had tried to kill him with his bushwacking cowhands. This didn't sit well with the young man, and he walked through the doors of the saloon to see Hubert and one of his men sitting at a table with a bottle of whiskey.

Brody took in a gulp of air and exhaled then walked to where Hubert sat.

"Your men failed to shoot me in the back tonight, Hubert. Stand up and let's see if you're man enough to do it, facing me."

Hubert's face got red, and he was sweating. "I don't know what you're talking about."

"You're not only a yellow belly, but a liar to go along with it. Now stand up and we settle this right here and now," said Brody, who saw the other man with Hubert ease his hand down to his gun. He was ready for the man to make the play.

Hubert kind of slid his chair back and reached out with his left hand to steady himself as he stood. Brody raised his hand up to his chest and inside his vest. When Hubert stood and removed his left hand off the table, he went for his gun.

Brody pulled the shoulder holster gun and shot Hubert in the face. Blood and bone exploded and then he turned to the other man who was bringing his gun up to shoot. Two quick shots to his chest, and the gunfight was over.

Brody reloaded his gun and turned to the crowd. "You all saw that they went for their guns first. I shot them in self-defense." He walked out of the saloon and headed to the livery stable.

The marshal was running toward the saloon, and Brody waited on him.

"Marshal, Hubert and one of his men are dead in the saloon. They drew on me, and I defended myself. I'm leaving town in a few minutes, and I'm sorry for all the gunplay that's happened."

The marshal looked at the young man and smiled. "It's been nice knowing you, Doctor. I hope you find what it is you're looking for in life."

"Thanks, Marshal." They shook hands, and he continued to the livery.

Chapter Thirty-Nine

THE LIVERYMAN HAD ALL BUT CLOSED UP FOR the night and was getting ready to go home when Brody walked in. "I'm sorry, but I'll be needing my horse tonight. I'm leaving town to go back home."

"It's kind of late and it's getting colder out to be traveling in the dark. Are you sure you want to leave tonight?"

Brody thought about what the man said and replied, "I do believe you're right. I'll go to the hotel for the night, but I have to leave by daylight. Is there a way I can have my horse ready to go by then?"

"Yep, I'll have your mount saddled and ready for you by daylight. I hate to see you go, young man. That's going to leave the town without a doctor."

"Actually, Dr. Stevens came back today. The town is in good hands once again."

The liveryman adjusted a suspender. "Dr. Stevens is a cantankerous cuss, but he does know what he's doing, I reckon."

"I'll be back in the morning," said Brody, and took his

bag with him to the hotel where he checked in and ordered a hot bath. He figured that this might be the last chance to properly bathe until he arrived in Wichita.

After the bath and wearing clean clothes, he walked to the saloon, and Lilly was in there waiting tables.

As soon as he sat down at an empty table, Lilly came over. "Hi Lilly, how are you doing?"

"I'm doing fine. I heard that you're leaving town."

"I'm going back to Kansas to go to medical school. I spoke to Dr. Stevens and he's well aware of your situation and he's agreed to watch after you."

She put her hand on his arm. "I appreciate that. I still wish it was you, but I understand you wanting to go off to school. You may not know this but you're now the fastest man alive from all the stories and lies coming from the saloon."

Brody had to laugh at what she said. "I didn't intend to ever be called a fast gun. Maybe those men were just really slow."

She sat down next to him. "I'm sure glad you're the one that's in here talking to me. I had no use for Hubert or his men. They were overbearing and tried to run roughshod with everyone when they got tanked up on whiskey."

"I saw right off that he was a bully, and I don't associate well with that sort of person." Brody pointed to the table where men were eating. "Do you have any food for sale?"

"I sure do. The stew is really good, or we have ham and potatoes."

Brody thought for a second. "I'll have some of both if that's all right."

Lilly got up. "I'll be right back with your food."

She brought him a plate of food along with a bowl of

hot stew. She then went back to serving drinks to the other customers.

Brody ate his meal and was at the door ready to leave the saloon when Lilly came and grabbed him by his arm.

"Brody, I just heard that there's two men at the other saloon in town looking for you. I suggest that you go ahead and leave town. The big one is Hubert's older brother, August, and the other one is his kin. They're filling up on a bottle of courage and will be looking for you soon."

Brody stood still for a few seconds and then asked, "You said there at the other saloon? Did the person who told you say where in the room they were at?"

Lilly pulled him by his arm over to where no one was at. "You can't be thinking about going in there. They'll kill you. August is meaner than Hubert ever was."

Brody took a deep breath and thought about what to do. "Listen, I can't be looking over my shoulder all the time. I don't want to do it, but I'll not let August or anyone else bird dog me. Can you send word to the girls over there to stay out of the line of fire when I come in, because I'm going in shooting and not give them a chance to shoot me."

"Oh, Dr. Brody, I wish you would reconsider this," said Lilly. "August wears a buffalo robe and usually stands at the bar drinking. You be very careful of him."

He smiled at Lilly. "I'll be fine. Go on now and send a warning to the girls at the other saloon."

Brody walked outside, pulled his gun, and checked the loads in the chambers. This was one of those times that he wished he had went on out where the herd was, but he would have to face this August feller sooner than later.

William had taught him to take the fight to his opponent. Don't give the enemy time to adjust or defend themselves. Be the aggressor and take the fight to August and that's what he was going to do.

Brody pulled the shoulder holster gun and put it in his left hand. The men would see the gun on his hip and wouldn't think about him having two guns. He held the gun by the grips behind his back and walked through the door of the saloon. He had to go some fifteen feet forward before he could come up behind the two men who had one boot on the foot rail and leaned on the bar top, kicking back shots of whiskey.

Brody stopped and pulled the hammer back on the gun he had concealed behind his back. "August, I hear that you're looking for me."

The big man turned his head far enough where he could see. "Are you the man that killed my brother?"

"That's right. He was an overbearing coward like you, and I shot him," said Brody, knowing that the man would probably make his play out of anger.

The big man clawed for his gun as he turned, but the young gun hand was one up on him and shot August three times in the chest before he could pull the gun from its holster.

The other man was much faster and got his first shot off that went into the floor of the saloon. He and Brody fired at the same time, and Brody felt the sting of the bullet as it grazed his arm. The other man was going to the floor and was dead by the time Brody checked for a pulse.

One of the barmaids came running up to the young doctor with a rag and put it against his left shoulder. "You've been hit and it's bleeding."

Brody looked at the wound. "I'll be all right. I think

Dr. Stevens can fix me up. It looks like I don't have to watch over my shoulder anymore."

Brody walked to the doctor's office holding the rag against his arm.

"Dr. Stevens, I need a little help if you don't mind."

The bullet cut a furrow in the skin about two inches above his left elbow. It looked much worse than it was, and the doctor fixed him up by putting iodine on the wound and tying a bandage around his arm.

"That arm's going to be sore for a few days. Take a few clean bandages with you and change them out every day or two."

"Thanks, Doctor. I'll be seeing you when I get out of medical school." Brody left the office and headed to the hotel. This had been a long day, and the next few days would be really long and exhausting.

The fatigued young man didn't even undress in the hotel room. He removed his boots, guns and laid on the bed.

Chapter Forty

BRODY WOKE UP STARTLED. HAD HE HEARD something that woke him from a deep sleep? With a gun in hand, he pulled open the door to find the hallway empty. He laid back down but knowing that it would be time to get up soon, he went ahead and washed his face from the pitcher of water by the washbasin. The arm where the bullet grazed him was really sore and ached. He kept working the arm to loosen it up.

The hotel clerk wasn't in the lobby, but the grandfather clock in the reception area showed that it was five in the morning. Brody popped his head inside the tiny dining room to find it also empty.

The café beside the saloon was lit up, and when he walked in, a different girl was working that morning.

"You want a cup of coffee while your breakfast is cooking?" she asked.

Brody shook his head. "No, a glass of milk would be good, though. I would also like ham and eggs for breakfast."

"Coming right up. A half dozen eggs fried or scrambled?"

"Fried if you don't mind."

The meal was more than he usually had for breakfast. This was the first time in his life that he ate six eggs at one time. He didn't know when his next meal would be so he figured he might as well stuff himself.

The livery was open when he arrived, and the owner had his horse fed and saddled. Brody handed the man some money. "Thanks for saddling my horse."

"No problem at all. If you're going to join up with that cattle drive then you need a pair of leather chaps to wear. They'll help keep you warm, but most importantly, they'll keep the thorns and branches from hitting your legs. I happen to have a pair that I'd sell you cheap," said the hostler.

"The mornings are getting colder every day now. I believe that I'll buy them from you, and if you have any gloves, I'll buy them also."

The hostler sold him the chaps, gloves, and two squares of material that he could use to cover his face from the dust off the trail, and a used rope made out of leather strands braided together.

Brody mounted up and started out of town. His horse was liking the cool morning and wanted to go faster than a walk. It was about four miles east until they intersected with the Chisholm Trail. The sound of the cattle lowing could be heard a good half mile before he rode upon the herd.

Delmer came riding up on his horse and said, "Today you'll ride drag. Chester is already back there, and he'll show you what to do. Now listen up. The main thing is to not get too close to the horns. Those cattle will come at you if you push them too close. I suggest you take a length of rope about ten feet long and use it to slap them on their butts. Follow me and I'll take you to the back of the herd."

Chester and Mitchel were both at what Delmer called the drag. Both men had their handkerchiefs over their mouths and noses. Brody did likewise and Chester came over to him.

"We'll be pushing the cattle to keep moving. You'll have to ride back and forth, hollering and slapping them with your rope to keep them going. Don't worry if one tries to leave the herd. We have out riders that will make them get back in line. I'm going to be to the left, and Mitchel will be on the right. You stay between us, but don't get too close to the cattle and wind up like Rufus."

Brody uncoiled a few wraps of his rope. "Do I start making them go now?"

"No, Delmer will let us know when he's ready for us to move out. All you have to do is be ready. They could be a little stubborn since we stayed an extra day letting them graze. Once we get them started they'll head on out since they're trail-wise."

Brody was glad he bought the chaps and gloves from the liveryman. In the saddle now for close to an hour in the cold was beginning to give him a chill. The chaps were keeping his legs warm. He tied another handkerchief around his neck and stuffed the loose material into his shirt.

They heard a noise up ahead, and the outriders started shouting at the cattle. Chester motioned with his arms and started hollering at the cattle. Brody watched as Chester and Mitchel rode down the line, swatting them with their ropes.

Brody did the same as his fellow drag riders, and the cattle started moving forward. A few wanted to chomp off a clump of little blue stems, but the slap of the ropes got their attention, and they fell in line.

The drive hadn't been started more than ten minutes before Brody realized why the cowboys all had their handkerchief covering their mouths and noses. The dust from the trampling cattle was covering the riders at the back of the herd. Sometimes it was hard to see for the dust, and what made matters worse was his eyes watering and mixing with the dust on his face.

The drag riders were covered in dirt by the time they came to the Cimmaron River shortly after midday. The men let the cattle have their fill of water, and that took extra time, but it also allowed Brody and the men with him to take turns going upstream to wash their faces and breathe fresh air. It also gave them time to swap to fresh horses since their mounts were tired and also covered in the dirt off the trail.

Once the cattle were across the river, Delmer came riding by letting everyone know that he wanted at least four more miles before they stopped for the night. That meant that the drovers would have to urge the cattle to go faster now that they had water, and some even had time to graze.

Delmer assigned another of the drovers to drop back and work drag with the other three. He wanted to push the cattle and get the miles he needed to stay on schedule. With the four of them slapping the rumps of the cattle, they were able to get the herd almost running toward where the wagon had headed to set up camp.

The herd traveled past Dover and were beginning to lose some of their energy when Delmer rode to the back and told each drag rider to keep putting pressure on the cattle, and they would bed down in about two more miles alongside a small creek north of Dover.

That was the best news that Brody had heard today. His left arm was sore and painful to the touch but it wasn't much he could do about it now. He figured it was from using it so much swinging the rope, hitting the cattle.

The sun was setting in the west when Delmer came to the back and told the riders to start letting the cattle slow down. The chuck wagon was just up ahead to the right, out of the way of the cattle.

When the cows started to mill around and graze, Brody and the men with him rode to where the camp was already set up and three fires were going so the men could get warm and eat their supper.

Brody unsaddled the horse he was riding and put his saddle close to one of the fires and went ahead and laid out his ground tarp and bedroll. He was so tired that all he wanted to do was eat supper and go to sleep.

The cook, who was called Crank, because he seemed to be mad all the time, had the men hot stew with corn bread and coffee which Brody declined and had water with his meal. When he had his belly full, he pulled off his boots and guns and climbed into his bed.

Delmer called out from the fire where he was sitting with some of the men.

"Brody, did you happen to see Hubert anymore after we left the other night?"

"Yeah, I saw him. He sent three of those men with him to bushwhack me when I went to see my girlfriend."

"Really, what happened?" asked Delmer.

"I killed them and then went into the saloon and had it out with Hubert and the other man with him. You won't be bothered by Hubert or his overgrown brother August ever again. They're both dead and buried," said Brody, and rolled over onto his side and went to sleep.

Chapter Forty-One

THE FOLLOWING MORNING, BRODY WOKE UP feeling a little feverish and sore all over. He wasn't used to being in the saddle all the time and his thighs and rump were feeling it when he stood up. The shoulder was extremely sore and that was a concern. After shaking out his boots to get rid of any squatters that wanted to make them their resident, he took the Indian pouches out and mashed together some of the leaves and herbs into a paste.

While sitting close to the fire for the light and warmth, he removed his shirt and threw the dirty bandage into the fire. The cool poultice felt good against the hot skin where the arm was red and showed signs of infection.

Delmer came up and pointed to Brody's arm. "That looks like a bullet wound. Did you get hit in that skirmish with Hubert?"

Brody continued to apply the medication. "No, I got hit by the man with August. I was lucky that he couldn't hit his target. In fact, his first shot was in the floor. I'm okay though and can do my job."

"I wouldn't expect anything less from you. Do you want me to put the bandage on for you?"

"I would appreciate that."

The men had breakfast and then got the cattle going. They let them have water when they crossed Little Turkey Creek south of Hennessee and then continued on north.

———

AROUND TWO THAT AFTERNOON, the herd started down into a valley and that's when the men started to get a little nervous. Up ahead on each side of the Chisholm Trail were about a dozen Indians with rifles.

Delmer stopped the cattle and could be seen riding down the right side of the herd saying something to the men. When he told Brody there were Indians up ahead and to be ready to fight, Chester came riding over to see what was going on.

Brody looked up ahead but couldn't see the Indians because of the dust. He wanted to see what they looked like and rode away from the side of the herd until he could see them. Remembering back to the time he spent with William and the family, where he did surgery on the sick woman's appendix, these Indians looked familiar.

This was decision time and he needed to talk to Delmer before the trail boss did anything. Chester was waiting on him when he returned to his place at the drag.

"What on earth are you up to, Brody?"

"I need to go talk to Delmer. I may be able to get us out of a bind since I spent some time not far from here with the Indians. If he'll let me go talk to them, I think we can pass without any shooting.

Chester moved his horse over a little. "Have at it, but you be ready for trouble if talking won't work."

Brody took off toward the front of the herd and found Delmer and four of the outriders watching the Indians.

Delmer had a somber look on his face when Brody rode up. "Brody, what're you doing up here?"

"I spent time with some Indians not far from here before I went to Kingfisher. Let me go talk to them and see what they want."

"I know what they want," said Delmer, taking his hat off and wiping his brow with his shirt sleeve. "They want this herd."

Brody shook his head slightly. "I don't think so. I think they would settle for a couple of cows to feed their people. If you'll let me talk to them, I'm almost certain that we can strike a deal."

Delmer shrugged his shoulders. "It's your life, but if anything goes wrong, we'll get the party started. I'll ride with you and all the men can back us up."

Brody and Delmer started toward the braves, and Delmer asked, "How do you know which one is in charge?"

"See the one on the gray with the white stockings and the medicine bag neckless around his neck? He's the medicine man and probably the one in charge or at least they'll listen to him. I can speak a little of their language so just listen unless I ask you a question."

"Fair enough," said Delmer.

As they rode closer, the medicine man made a circle motion with his hand, and the braves walked their horses forward, but he didn't move. They were instructed to encircle the two white men.

Brody stopped his horse and raised his left hand. "Dogotee, migebo mindee of William Longtooth." Then he pulled out the leather pouches that William had given him before he left some months past.

The Indian looked at Brody and smiled with a toothless mouth. "Are you the healer called Brody Connor?"

"I am Brody Connor, and I have strong medicine that William taught me. It is in my healing pouch and in my guns. We come through here in peace and respect the land that the Great Spirit has provided to our native brothers. What is it that you want from us?" Brody moved his horse closer to the medicine man.

The man rubbed his stomach. "We ask for cows to fill the bellies of our people."

Brody looked at Delmer and then at the Indian. "What are you called?"

"I am Cache, the Healer of my tribe. My people are hungry for meat."

Brody motioned for Delmer to move forward. "This is Delmer. He owns these cows and he's a friend to the Apache. He is offering you four cows to take back to your people."

The young man who was to Cache's left moved forward and shouted out, "We take them all."

Brody pulled his pistol and pointed it at the young brave. "You take cattle and you die first. This is my medicine, and there is no dickering." He never took his eyes off the young brave when he asked, "Cache, do we have a deal?"

The older and wiser man asked, "Delmer, can we have six cows? That will feed us for a few weeks."

Delmer rode up beside the medicine man. "I am a good friend of the Apache and will give you eight cows so your people have full bellies." Then he stuck out his hand, and the two men shook hands.

Brody still had his gun on the young brave until Cache moved his horse over beside the young brave and spoke to him in his native tongue. Then, Cache rode to Brody and stuck out his arm in a friendly manner. Brody took hold of the man's forearm, and the Indian did likewise.

"Healer, you are welcome at my table anytime. I will tell William that I saw you today and we will thank the Great Spirit together for your leadership."

"Thank you, Cache. Where is your home located?"

"I am south of the house where you healed my brother's daughter."

Brody smiled. "How's she doing?"

"Very good. You have strong medicine to heal her. I tried, but the Great Spirit didn't hear me. He heard you and directed your knife."

Brody stuck out his hand again. "Thank you, my friend. We go get your cows now so you can feed your families."

Chapter Forty-Two

DELMER AND BRODY RODE BACK WHERE THE men were watching, and Delmer gave an order. "A couple of you cut out eight of the older cows and drive them over to the Indians. The rest of you get the herd moving before they change their minds."

Brody started to the back of the herd but was stopped when Delmer called out, "Brody, help take the cows to Cache. I'm sure he would like that."

Brody only nodded and helped to drive the cows where the braves were waiting on them. He tipped his hat to Cache and rode back to the back of the herd to help get the cattle going again.

That evening, when they had bedded down for the night and had their supper, Delmer came and sat down beside Brody.

"That was a brave thing you did today, especially when that young brave wanted to start something. You were mighty fast pulling that pistol."

"Yeah, I knew it would stop him, and Cache didn't want to start something that would get a good portion of his men hurt. I learned from the Indian that I stayed with for three months about how they fight and that surprise and numbers are their biggest offense. Today, they had neither, especially after I had the brave covered. Cache knew that I could kill at least two or three of his men before they could get in the fight. He didn't like those odds."

"Well, giving away eight cows was a small price to pay to not have trouble and stampede the herd. You did good today. Now get some rest," said Delmer as he walked away.

Brody went to his bedroll and crawled in. He didn't realize how exhausted he was until the next morning when one of the other cowboys had to wake him up.

It seemed like he hadn't rested at all that night by the way his tired and aching body felt. Although his arm was much better and some of the soreness had finally left. He made himself get his boots, guns, and hat on before he did something that he never did, he drank coffee that morning with his bacon and biscuits. After two cups of the scalding black liquid, he saddled up his horse and went to the rear of the herd.

That day, after two cold biscuits and bacon for his noon meal, he rode over to Chester. "I've been watching you with that rope. Would you show me how to use a rope to catch a cow?"

"Yeah, I'll show you some of the important things and you'll have to find your own rhythm and then practice throwing a loop," said Chester, and removed the coil of rope. "First, you have to know how to build a loop. The eye is called the Hondo. Grab the rope between the spoke, which I like to hold about eighteen inches from the eye. Hold the coil in your left hand and keep the tail in with your elbow up. I use my wrist to let the loop sail toward the cow."

"Will you show me again how you make the loop and how much lead you have before you throw the rope?" asked Brody.

Chester showed him again and then they had to urge some of the cattle forward. When they had time, Chester came over. "It's your time to start practicing what I showed you. Build your loop and then start swinging it toward the cow you want to rope."

The new roper started trying to replicate how Chester made his loop and then began to swing the loop over his head. The action was so out of kilter that the rope caught on his neck.

Chester started to laugh and then said, "Don't hold your hand so high. Hold the loop away from your body a little more and use the wrist to control the action of the loop. When it feels comfortable, throw it at something on the ground."

Brody began to practice his swing and then throwing the loop on saplings they passed by. A few times he even caught one. By the time they bedded down that night, his arms were tired from all the extra throwing.

That night, he was assigned to ride herd from midnight to three in the morning. He had never done that before and getting out of his warm bed at midnight was almost too much for the young man. He had to wear all his warm clothes as he rode around the herd, letting them know they couldn't wander off into the night.

When it was time to swap out to the next rider, Brody only pulled off his boots and guns before getting back to sleep. When he woke up to the cook making breakfast, he was finally warm and had coffee again that morning.

He was able to practice his roping ability that morning and that afternoon he rode to Chester and asked, "Would it be all right if I rope some of the calves?"

"Sure, but just remember that if you catch one you'll have to dismount and remove the rope from their head."

Brody looked a little puzzled. "I'm not sure how to do that. They won't stay still until I get the rope off, will they?"

"I'll show you one time and then it's all up to you." Chester made himself a loop and then went after a calf of about two hundred pounds. He landed the loop on the first throw and wrapped the slack around the horn before dismounting and followed the rope to the calf. He grabbed the rope with one hand and the calf's flank with the other and threw it to the ground. With his knee on the neck, he removed the rope and the calf got up and ran off.

Chester was coiling up his rope and came over to Brody. "That's how it's done. I would make sure not to pick out one bigger than you can handle."

Brody threw at one and was way short of his mark. The second one, the rope landed on the back of the calf. He made his loop and went over where a calf was beside the cow and threw the loop. Lo and behold, it landed over the horns of the cow, and when he took up the slack, she turned and started toward his horse. Brody almost panicked but spurred his horse so it would take off.

The big problem was, he couldn't separate from the cow since his rope was still on it. Chester came riding up and threw his rope, catching the hind legs of the cow, and she went down onto the ground.

Chester dismounted and rushed to the cow so he could hold her head down while his horse kept tension on the back legs. She was thrashing with the front ones, trying to get up.

"Brody, make your horse put pressure on the rope, and you get over here and get this darn rope off before she gets loose."

Brody backed his horse up and then he rushed over to the cow and removed the rope off one horn. She got her front footing and started up and that's when he got the rope clear and ran back to his horse.

Chester was also running and made it back before the cow's hind legs came clear of his rope. The cow stood looking at the two men, and Brody spoke out, "I think I made her a little mad."

"You reckon," said Chester. "You almost got in a real bind a few minutes ago. Don't be roping anymore calves when they're beside their mama."

"Yes, sir. That was a close one, all right." Brody turned his horse and went back to work.

That night at supper, the cook came over and started putting more food on Brody's plate. "I figure you need a little more substance if you're going to rope wild long-horns tomorrow."

The men started laughing, and all the young man could do was laugh with them. He didn't let the extra food go to waste. It hit the spot that night and he again had to ride night herd.

Chapter Forty-Three

THE FOLLOWING TWO DAYS WENT BY WITHOUT any incidents with Brody practicing his roping skills. He was able to rope some of the smaller animals and learned how to take them down so he could get the rope off.

But on the third day, when he lassoed a young calf and dismounted to get the rope off, the mother came at him ready to fight. He was able to run away from the calf, and when the cow turned to go see about her baby, he hurried to his horse and mounted back up. He untied the tail of the rope and spurred his horse forward enough so he could slap the cow across her nose with the braided leather. She took off running to get away, and he was able to get his rope off the calf.

That afternoon, the herd came to the Salt Fork of the Arkansas River.

Delmer came round and told everyone to get the cattle across and then they would bed down for the night. What he didn't tell them was that it would take the rest of the day to get them across the red water.

That night, as the men sat around the fire drinking

coffee, Delmer stood and got everyone's attention. "Tomorrow we'll be in Kansas. We should be in Wichita in four days. So let's keep our heads in the game and no one gets hurt."

Brody was learning each day about being a cowboy, and the men were all friendly to him. He didn't want to think about what he would do when he arrived in Wichita. Even though riding drag was easy, there were many times a man could be injured if he didn't keep his mind on the work. Cows had a temper and could turn on a horse and rider for no reason.

Brody didn't know when the herd crossed the border into Kansas the following day, but that night, the men were more laid back than normal. Brody thought the change was due to the drovers knowing that the end of the drive was near.

Delmer had the men push the herd harder the next three days. On the fourth day, the trail boss rode on ahead of the herd to notify the cattle pens. Brody and the rest of the men were ready for the drive to be over. Riding drag had taught him some valuable lessons, but his future wasn't going to be looking at the rear end of cattle.

Delmer rode back and helped the men guide the cattle into pens where the buyers would make a tally of the herd. Brody, Chester, and Mitchel headed to the water pump and ran water over their heads to wash away some of the dirt.

The men went back to where Crank parked the chuckwagon. The remuda was close by, grazing when Delmer came riding up. He dismounted and said to the men, "I made a good deal on the cattle. Any of you besides Brody want to call it quits, now's the time, so I can pay you off. As for the rest of you, I'll give each man twenty dollars and you can spend the night in town. I'll give you the rest of your pay when we get home."

Delmer walked to Brody and handed him twenty dollars. "Here, you earned this, eating all that dust. I appreciate you helping out me and the boys and I wish you the best going to doctor school."

"Thanks, boss man," said Brody, and shook hands with Delmer. He made his way to each man and shook hands before he mounted up.

On the way into town, Brody thought about where he would go and what he would do. His mama was on his mind, and the young man didn't know if it would be safe for her if he went to her house. He wanted to take a hot bath and change into clean clothes.

While thinking about his next move, Brody decided to rent a room at the hotel so he could clean up there. The clothes in his bag were probably soiled with dust off the trail drive. He would certainly need more clothes when he went off to medical school.

With his hat pulled down to shield as much of his face as possible, Brody rode past the tavern that Ludwig had owned. He wanted to stop and go inside but thought better of it until he knew more about Ludwig's brother. The cowboy didn't know the man's name, but that wouldn't be a problem finding out.

Brody stopped in front of the emporium where he left his horse and went inside. Men's britches were on a table to the right of the door and that's where Brody was when a man came to him. "Are you looking for new britches?"

Brody made eye contact. "Yes, I am. I want two new pairs, two shirts, socks, and undergarments."

The man helped Brody pick out his clothing, and with them wrapped in butcher paper and tied with twine, he continued to the hotel. He was able to rent a room, and the clerk was getting his bath ready while he took his horse to the livery stable. The hostler looked at Brody kind of strange but didn't say anything as he took the horse inside.

Brody returned to the hotel to clean up before he went out. The bath and a shave did wonders, and he felt great being clean and wearing new clothing. He wanted to see his mama, but he needed to know a few details first.

Brody opened the door to Dr. Melrose's medical practice and went inside. He didn't see his former employer, and he called out, "Dr. Melrose, are you here?"

"Thaddeus, is that you?" asked the physician as he came from the back room.

"Yep, it's me, but I changed my name to Brody," said the young man, and stuck out his hand to the doctor.

"You can give me a hug, young man. I'm really glad to see you."

"Thanks, Dr. Melrose, it's good to see you."

"Thad, I mean Brody, have you seen your mama?"

Brody shook his head. "No, not yet. I wanted to talk to you first. Do you know anything about Ludwig's brother?"

"It's been a difficult time for your ma. Hermon is Ludwig's brother and he's taken over the tavern and your ma has to work for him. He's just as mean as Ludwig and the tavern is not more than a den of hoodlums that rob and beat people. You have to be careful around Hermon. He's killed two men since he's been in town. Both times he had witnesses that claim he shot them in self-defense."

"What does Hermon look like, and how will I recognize him?"

"Hermon must be six foot four and weighs close to

three hundred pounds. Don't underestimate his ability based on his size. He wears a gun on his hip but has a backup gun in a shoulder holster. He also has a man overseeing the bar and gambling who has already killed at least two men since he's lived in Wichita. He came here with Herman after Ludwig died. As for recognizing Hermon, he wears a ring in his right ear," said the doctor.

"What about the man who runs the bar? What does he look like?"

"I don't think I've ever seen him, but I've seen his handiwork using his hands and feet. I was told that he is bald-headed with a bushy beard. Brody, do not underestimate this man at all. I've treated at least five men he beat inside the tavern and like I already said, I know of two men he shot."

"What about my ma. Has Hermon beat her like Ludwig did?"

"I haven't treated her if that's what you're asking?" said Dr. Melrose. "I only know what I've heard from other patients. I've been told that she started out trying to run the tavern, but the bartender was stealing her blind. When she tried to do something about it, Herman came to town and took over. The only way she could earn money from the business was waiting tables."

Brody took a deep breath. "I was afraid Elmer would try to steal from her. I told him what would happen if he did. I reckon he thought the two men Hermon sent to kill me would finish the job and he would get away with it."

Dr. Melrose came and put his hand on the boy's shoulder. "Brody, I hope you head on up to Kansas City and get enrolled in classes. Going to the tavern could jeopardize you going to medical school. I highly suggest you leave the men at the tavern alone. Your mama is dealing with it and as far as I know, she's healthy. Go home and talk to your mother, she may want to go with you."

"Thanks, Doctor, I'm leaving to go see my mama. I just needed a little insight on what's going on around here before I saw her," said Brody, and shook his friend's hand.

Brody walked toward his house, and as he approached the residence, no light could be seen. The door was locked, but the key was in the hidden place under the mat. Brody opened it and walked inside to find the house empty after looking in each room. He sat down in the dark and thought about his next move.

Chapter Forty-Four

SITTING IN THE DARK HOUSE GAVE BRODY TIME to process what Dr. Melrose told him about Hermon, his right-hand man, and the bartender. He couldn't walk into the tavern and start shooting, but he could start building a plan. William had taught him to be the aggressor, be in control by planning the attack, take the enemy by surprise, and know the movements of the enemy.

Brody had the plan in his head when he locked the front door and walked to the tavern. The walk gave him time to make sure his guns were free to use in case there was trouble.

When the young man entered the block where the tavern was located, music could be heard coming from down the street. As he got closer to the tavern, he stayed in the shadows as much as he could until he stopped at the window.

Staying hidden as much as he could, Brody peered into the dirty window with the hopes of seeing his mama. She wasn't immediately visible, but he did see the bartender and the man that he thought was the manager. The man's bald head and beard wasn't the only thing that got Brody's attention. The man had massive arms exposed by a shirt that was sleeveless.

The next observation of the man was where he was sitting. He was seated at the far end of the counter where he could see the entire room. From where Brody stood, he couldn't distinguish if the man was wearing a gun or not. That wasn't a large concern right now.

Brody moved back from the window and walked out into the street so he could walk past the front of the tavern without being seen. He made his way to the window on the opposite side he was previously at. While scanning the room, his mama came into view and started gathering empty glasses and bottles.

She seemed to be moving slowly as she worked, but he couldn't see her face. When she finally looked up, the shiner around her right eye disturbed Brody so much that he wanted to walk in and start shooting, but he was afraid his mama could be hurt.

Hermon still hadn't been seen inside the tavern, so the young man turned away from the window and walked to the hotel.

Sleep didn't come quickly for the future doctor. He kept thinking about the black eye his poor mother had when he saw her waiting tables. Brody made a promise to himself and to the woman who raised him that night. Never again would she be a punching bag for overbearing men.

———

THE FOLLOWING MORNING, Brody sat at the window of the café across the street from the tavern eating breakfast. He had a clear view of the entire block so he could see who came to the bar. The meal was finished, but the young man was still sipping on a glass of milk when he saw Elmer, the bartender, turn the corner and walk toward the tavern before sitting down on a bench.

Brody's first thoughts were for his safety. Had someone recognized him in town and Elmer was waiting on backup to approach the café. Then he saw the bar manager coming from the opposite end of the street. Brody placed his hand inside his vest in anticipation of trouble.

Elmer got up from the bench and joined the bar manager as he unlocked the door. The two men went inside, and Brody stayed where he was with the hopes of seeing Hermon.

Brody sat another thirty minutes and was getting ready to leave when he saw his mother over a block away. He hurried to the door and angled his path across the street to intercept her before she arrived at the tavern.

Ellen looked up and then she started to cry and put her right hand over her mouth. Brody made a sideward motion with his hand, indicating for his mother to go in the space between two buildings. Only a few feet inside the space, Ellen turned and threw open her arms.

"I didn't think I would ever see you again, my son."

"I know. I'm on my way to medical school, and I want you to come with me."

Ellen scowled. "I'm not sure that's a good idea. Ludwig's brother took the tavern away from me and has men looking for you. I'm scared he'll kill you if he gets a hint that you're here."

Brody touched the discolored skin beneath her right eye. "Who hit you?"

"Thaddeus, it's okay. You don't need to worry about this. It'll go away in a few more days."

"Mama, I changed my name to Brody Connor in case anyone was after me and it's important to me who hit you. Did Hermon hit you?"

She looked down at the ground and shrugged her shoulders. "No, it was Butch, the manager. Hermon has strict rules about breaking glasses and keeping the tables clean. I tripped and spilled four glasses of whiskey, and Butch backhanded me."

Brody looked toward the tavern. "Is that Butch inside with Elmer?"

"Thaddeus, promise me you won't try anything with Butch. He's twice as mean as Ludwig ever was. I've seen him cut three men with a straight razor and laugh while doing it."

Brody took her hand into his. "Mama, call me Brody. If someone hears my real name, there could be trouble before I can leave town. When does Hermon come to the tavern?"

"He should be there now. He lives in the back room and hardly ever comes into the main room. Butch runs the gambling and liquor business."

"Does Elmer work every day or does someone else give him a day off each week?"

"Elmer is off tomorrow, and Butch will tend to the bar. We usually ain't busy on Tuesdays."

"Mama, you best be on your way." Brody hugged his mother. "I don't want you getting in trouble for being late."

He turned and walked out of the space and started up the street. When he looked back, his mother was going inside the tavern.

Tomorrow would be the best time to pay Butch and

Hermon a visit. He knew where Elmer lived and would deal with him later. Right now, he wanted to go see his friend, Dr. Melrose and see if the man had time to answer some medical questions.

Chapter Forty-Five

BRODY ENTERED THE DOCTOR'S OFFICE WHERE the older physician was putting instruments in a pan of alcohol. "Good morning, Dr. Melrose."

"Hello, Thaddeus. I'm sorry, I meant Brody. What brings you by here this morning?"

"I wanted to ask you what books I'll need for my studies in medical school. I'd like to study until I arrive there with the hope that I won't be behind the rest of the class."

The reception office door opened and a female cried out. "Help! I need help!"

Brody took off to the reception area to find a beautiful woman holding onto the back of a chair. She was dressed in black leather britches, black boots, a violet shirt with a black vest, and wearing a black hat. On her right hip was a .41 caliber pistol.

"What's wrong?" questioned Brody as he walked up to her.

"I'm sicker than a dog. I'm hurting so bad that I'm throwing up. Please help me."

By that time, Dr. Melrose was in there with the woman and Brody. "Let's get her on the examination table and see what the problem is."

The two men led her to the table, where they, along with her helping, had the woman lying down. Brody immediately began to press on her abdomen and right side. At one particular location, she screamed out in pain and grabbed hold of his arm. "Don't push there. It hurts really bad," she screamed out.

Dr. Melrose stood watching Brody examine the woman. "What do you think it is, Brody?"

"I suggest we operate and see if it's her appendix or the gallbladder. She complained about throwing up, so I'm inclined to go with gallbladder," said Brody.

"I agree with that diagnosis," said Dr. Melrose and began his own examination. Again, the woman screamed out in pain when he touched one particular place.

"What are you going to do, Doctor?" asked the woman.

"We'll give you medicine that will put you to sleep and then we'll operate and remove whatever is causing you pain," said Dr. Melrose. He looked at Brody and said, "Go get water heating and get those hands scrubbed."

Brody was surprised. "You want me to help you operate?"

"I want to watch you in action, Dr. Brody," said his mentor.

Brody looked at the smiling, older doctor and realized this was his moment to show off what he had learned at the Indian woman's house.

"I'll get the water heating and get everything prepared for the surgery," said Brody, and started out of the room, but the doctor stopped him.

"I want you to get our patient ready, and I'll collect the instruments."

Brody went to the woman. "Ma'am, I'm Brody. I need to get you into that room over there." He pointed to the room to his left.

"I'm not sure if I can walk over there. I'm not feeling very good right now."

"What's your name?"

"It's Jennifer Bernie, and I brought a herd of cattle up here from Central Texas. I started hurting yesterday and —" She stopped talking because of the pain. Brody placed one arm under her neck and the other under her knees. He lifted her up and carried the moaning woman into the operating room.

Brody didn't wait on Dr. Melrose and got started by placing a sheet over her before he removed her clothing. "Miss Jennifer, I'm sorry, but I have to get your clothing off and clean the area where the doctor will make the incision."

Dr. Melrose came in. "I'll help you get her ready. Go ahead and get the chloroform prepared." The two men worked together getting her prepped and when they were ready to get started, Brody took over, making the incision and opening the area where he could work as Dr. Melrose assisted.

A little over an hour later, Jennifer opened her eyes and smiled at Brody. "I hurt but in a different way. Thank you, Dr. Brody."

The young man reached out and patted her on the arm. "Thank you for coming here today. I'm leaving here soon to enter medical school, and this was good schooling for me. You lay still, and I'll give you some laudanum to ease the pain and discomfort. Do I need to notify someone about your condition?"

"If you don't mind. My crew is south of town waiting on the shipping pens to get empty. My father's name is Big Joe. You can't miss him."

Brody gave her the medication and went to find Dr. Melrose.

"I'm riding out to her herd and to tell Jennifer's pa her condition and where she is. I'm sure he's worried about his daughter. Is there anything you need me to do?"

"No, but I would like to know what you're planning to do with Hermon?"

Brody decided to go ahead and tell his friend. "I found out that Butch hit my mama because she spilled a couple of glasses of whiskey. Butch will be in the tavern by himself in the morning and that's when I'm going to have a talk with him."

"I don't know what *have a talk with him* implies," said the doctor. "I want you to go in there and do whatever you have to do. I'll cover your back with the law."

Brody hugged the doctor and walked out without saying anymore. He knew what Dr. Melrose was saying and left the rest unsaid.

He found the herd two miles south of Wichita, and Jennifer was right. Her pa was a big man, tall and wide. Big Joe rode back with Brody and went to see his daughter while Brody put his horse in the livery stable.

It was getting close to darkness when he walked to the same café where he ate breakfast that morning. He was able to sit at the same table and watch who went in and out of the tavern.

Not many customers entered the bar, and after twenty minutes, Butch, the manager, came out and walked down the street to one of the other saloons. "Why was the man doing that?"

Brody had to know and took a couple more bites before he laid money on the table and walked out. He crossed over to the other side of the street and made his way to the saloon.

Brody practiced his training and let his eyes adjust to the dim lighting before he walked to the bar counter and ordered a beer. Shifting his eyes from right to left, Butch was nowhere to be seen.

The young man lifted the mug with his left hand and turned so he could see the entire room. Butch was sitting with another man at the table in the corner of the room. He watched as Butch pulled a paper from his shirt and handed it to the man.

The man looked at the paper, wadded it up, and threw it on the floor. Butch got up and headed to the door. The other man got up and walked toward the back door.

Brody walked over to the table and picked up the paper and walked outside where he opened it. *Send two more men after the boy. Hermon.*

Brody smiled, Hermon would get a surprise soon, and the man may not like it. Now it was time to look inside the tavern and see what was going on.

He had only been standing where he could see inside when a boy ran up to him. "Are you Brody?"

"Yeah. Who wants to know?"

"Dr. Melrose sent me after you. He said he needs help at the office."

"Do you know why?"

"It must be the woman. He said to find you and tell you to come quick."

Brody walked past the tavern and then started to run toward the doctor's office. He heard the doctor before he saw him and ran into the room where Jennifer was in agony.

Dr. Melrose had the bandage off the woman's incision and was in the process of cleaning the area.

"Brody, she's bleeding internally and we need to open her back up."

Brody went to Jennifer and started to press along the incision. "I did a similar operation on an Indian woman while I was gone, and I seared the area where I removed the appendix."

"Let's get busy and see if we can save this woman's life," said the doctor.

Dr. Melrose let Brody do the repair work, and he assisted. After it was over and Jennifer was resting. Dr. Melrose said, "Brody, you're going to make a fine physician someday. I'm impressed with the skills you have, and I'm going to send another letter to the medical school."

"Thanks, Doctor. I had a good teacher and was able to read a few books. If it's all right with you, I'll stay here and look after Jennifer until I know she's doing better."

Chapter Forty-Six

BRODY WENT INTO DR. MELROSE'S OFFICE AND found a medical book on the skeletal system that he could study. With a comfortable chair in the room with Jennifer, he began to read.

Darkness came, and Dr. Melrose sent Brody away to eat and then to the hotel for rest. The patient was doing much better, and Dr. Melrose said he would check on her during the night.

Brody went to the same café for his supper so he could spy on the tavern. The place seemed busy tonight, and he assumed that Jennifer's pa's herd had come to town since the hitchrail in front of the tavern as well as the saloon down the street were full.

After supper, the young man walked to the front of the tavern again and looked through the window. There weren't as many men inside as he first thought. While watching, two men rose from one of the poker tables and were exchanging words when Butch came over and hit one of the men on the side of his head so hard that the man hit the floor and lay there unconscious.

Butch had a powerful arm and Brody made a mental note not to face the man with a fist. As the muscular man turned, the jacket he wore opened enough for Brody to see the gun tucked away in a shoulder holster similar to his.

Butch motioned with his arm to someone that Brody couldn't see. It was his ma, and she was making her way to the unconscious man with a wet rag. Ellen kneeled beside the man and began to wash his face when Butch stepped beside her and slapped her on the back of her head. Brody couldn't hear what the man was saying to his mother, but the mere action caused Brody to start biting his lower lip. He backed away from the window, leaned his back against the wall, and closed his eyes while taking in deep breaths of air. He wanted to go inside and shoot Butch full of holes but refrained from letting his emotions dictate his actions.

Brody couldn't walk away knowing that his ma was being mistreated by the bully. He made his way back to the window and saw his mother pour a glass of water on the man's face. The man didn't move as the water was poured on him. Brody knew the water wouldn't work, but that was what people thought had to be done to wake someone up.

Two patrons went to the man and helped raise him into a sitting position which got a movement from the feller. With the help of a cowboy, they raised the man off the floor and started to drag him to the door. Brody moved away from the window and watched as the men sat the dazed man against the front wall and then they went back inside.

Brody wanted his mama out of the tavern so he could maneuver inside the business without worrying about her getting hurt. The sound of a gunshot brought him out of his thoughts. He ran to the window to see his ma on the floor. A man he didn't know was holding the gun on Butch as two cowboys got his mama off the floor. She was still unconscious as they carried her to the door. The man pointing the gun at Butch walked backward to the door, and Brody watched to make sure that Butch didn't try to follow. The bar manager started to laugh and walked back to the counter.

Brody followed the men who were carrying his mama up the boardwalk. They turned down the street that went to the doctor's office. Brody ran forward and caught up with the men. "What did Butch do to Ellen?"

He was mad at her over something and hit her with the leather-covered club he carries in his back pocket. She probably has a concussion from the lick.

"I'll go get Dr. Melrose up," said Brody, and took off running.

The door was still unlocked, and the doctor was in the room with Jennifer when Brody came in.

"A couple of men are bringing my mama here. She was hit by Butch with the club he carries in his pocket."

"Get her on in and we'll have a look. I'm thinking she may have a concussion, but we need to make sure."

After Ellen came awake, the doctor made his decision to keep her at his office a few days until he was certain that she could function without difficulty. Brody slept in a chair that night, and the next morning he went to the café for food. His mother needed to eat and so did Jennifer.

On his way back with food, he saw Elmer, the bartender, go inside the mercantile. Brody dropped off the food and headed back toward the main part of town and arrived in time to see Elmer walking toward the residential part of town.

Brody followed and saw the man go inside a small house. The door was open, and the young man could see that someone was inside the kitchen. He opened the screen door and rushed into the kitchen where Elmer turned around with a butcher knife in his hand.

The young man stood poised to draw his gun. "Hello, Elmer. I warned you what would happen when I shot Ludwig. You stole from my ma and then sided with Hermon and Butch."

"Boy, you're about to be cut up like a piece of meat," said Elmer, and stepped toward the boy. Brody bit his lower lip and pulled his gun without thinking about it. In a heartbeat, the gun was out of the holster and pointed at Elmer's face.

Elmer dropped the knife and ran toward the back door. Brody couldn't shoot the man in the back and started after him, only to see Elmer get on a horse that was already saddled.

"Stop, Elmer, or I'll shoot," shouted Brody.

The bartender didn't pay him no mind and kept going.

Brody holstered his weapon and stood there thinking. He would have to run to the livery after his horse. Elmer would have a good twenty-minute lead on him. If he didn't go after the man, Elmer would tell Hermon he was in town and that would do damage to his plan.

Brody took off running to the livery to get his horse. He worked as fast as he could, getting his pony saddled. Then went to the last place in town where he saw Elmer. All he could do was stay on the same street and hope the man hadn't turned and went in a different direction.

Four blocks from the last place he had seen Elmer, two elderly men were sitting under a tree, sharpening knives on a stone. Brody pulled up. "Howdy, men. Did you happen to see Elmer come by on his horse?"

One of the men stopped what he was doing and pointed south. "He came by here and turned south. I reckon he's going to the Anderson home place three miles south and a quarter east."

"Much obliged for the information," said Brody, and headed out, but not as fast as he had been going. Now that he knew where Elmer was heading, he could take his time and give the man time to think he got away.

Brody was about three miles south and saw a lane heading east. He could see the tops of a building, but that was all because of the timber between him and the structure. Riding past the lane for a good quarter of a mile and then turning east, brought him to the timber that lined both sides of a creek.

The creek didn't have much water in it, so he rode in it until he thought he was close enough to see the house. Leaving the horse in the timber, Brody made his way where he could see the house, barn, chicken pen, and outhouse.

He was ready to move when he saw Elmer come out of the house with a pistol in his hand walking to the outhouse. Brody stayed still when the bartender stopped and looked around before entering the one-hole privy.

Brody gave him time to get situated and started walking toward the tiny structure. He circled around to the side where the door hinged and waited. He could hear Elmer inside grunting, and in a few moments, the door opened, and the man stood looking at the lane and timber.

He still had the gun in his hand when he stepped away and turned to close the door. Elmer stopped and was bringing up the gun when Brody pulled leather and fired at the man who stole from his mama.

Elmer took two slugs to the chest and went down onto his knees. "I thought Hermon had you killed." Brody fired one more bullet that hit the bartender in the heart. He fell over dead.

Brody ejected the three spent shells and walked to the barn for a shovel and pickax.

The better part of two hours were spent digging the grave and rolling the corpse in it. If someone wanted to come looking, they may find the body if they worked for it.

Chapter Forty-Seven

ELMER MADE IT EASY FOR THE YOUNG MAN TO seek his revenge. Brody hadn't originally intended to kill the man, but had no choice when Elmer was pointing his gun at him. His plan was still in place for Butch and Hermon and it didn't have to happen today like he originally thought.

After dropping off his horse back at the livery stable, Brody once again walked to Dr. Melrose's office to check on his mama. She was still in bed, but was talking to Jennifer when he walked in.

"I see you two beautiful ladies have gotten acquainted," said Brody. "Mama, how are you feeling?"

"I'm still a little woozy when I sit up or try to stand. How are you?"

"I'm great now that I know you're going to be okay." He turned to Jennifer. "How are you feeling?"

"I'm sore and my side hurts when I move, but I'm way better today than I was yesterday when I came in here. Your mama has been trying to fix me and you up," said Jennifer, smiling.

Brody leaned on her bed. "Well, that wouldn't be the worst thing that ever happened to you, Miss Jennifer, but I'm leaving for medical school after I take care of my business here in Wichita."

Ellen cleared her throat. "Thaddeus, I mean Brody. You need to leave them men alone and get on the road to Kansas City. I can take care of myself."

"I can see that, Mama, but I wouldn't be much of a man if I rode off now, would I? You stay put here and I'll see to my business when I feel it's the best time."

Jennifer chimed in on the conversation. "Are you any good with that hog leg?"

"I can hold my own."

"If you want some help, I'm sure I can talk my daddy into helping, and he'll bring the cowboys along to help the man that saved my life."

"I appreciate the notion, but I can handle what I have to do."

"Son, you don't know anything about fighting and especially when it comes to gunplay. I've seen Butch and Hermon in action, and they're mean men. Butch is brutal with his fist, club, and that knife he carries. Hermon's fast with his gun, and he don't mess around. If he even thinks there's going to be gunplay, he don't wait around, he gets the ball rolling."

Brody stood up and started to pace the floor. "While I was gone, I met an old Indian man, and he took me in and taught me how to fight and shoot. I'm not the same kid that left here months ago. Mama, I've killed men along the way, and I'll never sit back and let men beat on you or any woman again. I made a promise to myself, never again would I let it happen."

"Son, these men are killers, and they won't think

twice about killing you or me. You have to leave here immediately before they know you returned."

"Mama, I have a plan, and I'll leave as soon as I can. Right now, I need for you to get well and stay away from the tavern. It's not safe for you there anymore."

Ellen hit the bed with her fist. "You don't understand. I have no other means of making a living. You can't go there and start a fight. Butch will beat you worse than Ludwig ever did."

"Mama, I promise you that I won't fight with Butch. I have a plan and when I'm finished, everything will be fine."

She reached out for her son, and he came to her. "Don't you lie to me. I don't want Butch beating you."

Brody leaned down. "I'm not fighting with Butch." He gave his mama a hug. "I have to go now and eat supper. I didn't eat any dinner, and my belly thinks my throat has been cut."

———

AFTER GOODBYES, Brody walked out of the doctor's office and walked toward the tavern. Once through the door, he stood for the longest time, letting his eyes adjust to the lighting.

Butch was behind the counter with a towel draped over his left shoulder, filling mugs with beer and shot glasses with whiskey when Brody took a spot at the end of the bar where he could see what the man was doing. When Butch looked at Brody, he pointed to a mug and then a glass. Brody called out, "Beer."

While Butch was busy with his work, Brody made sure both of his guns were free to draw. Butch delivered the beer. "That's twenty cents."

Brody flipped a quarter onto the countertop while biting his bottom lip. Butch picked it up, and as he did, Brody moved to his left where he was clear of the counter, and said, "It's time you pay for hitting my mama."

Butch spun around and was pulling his gun from the shoulder holster when Brody pulled his gun and fired one shot that entered Butch's right eye and exited out the back of his head. Blood, bone, and brain matter flew through the air, covering the counter and bottles of liquor.

Brody turned toward the room with the gun still in his hand. "He went for his gun, and I shot in self-defense." He turned and went to the door that opened into the back room. Hermon was nowhere to be found.

Brody came back into the main room and two men were going through Butch's pockets. "You men get away from him. Whatever money that he has and what's in the cash can belongs to my ma, and I'll kill anyone that steals from her."

The men walked away from Butch and in walked two city deputies with their guns drawn. "Who killed Butch?"

Brody raised his left hand. "That would be me. As you can see by the gun in his hand, he was pulling on me when I shot him in self-defense. All these men saw it and will tell you the truth."

One of the deputies looked around the room at the heads going up and down. He then asked, "Where is the owner of the place?"

Brody spoke up and replied, "She's at Dr. Melrose's office recuperating from a concussion."

"I was asking for Hermon," said the deputy. "He's the man in charge."

Brody shouted out, "Anyone know where Hermon is?"

The dealer at the poker table spoke, "He went to McPherson three days ago. I don't recall when he's coming back."

"Do you know why he went to McPherson?" asked Brody.

"Not really, but I suspect he has a family up there and farmland."

Brody went to the deputy who seemed to be in charge. "Am I free to go?"

"Yeah, you can go about your business. A word of advice. You should leave town and not cause any more trouble."

"Thanks," said Brody, and walked out of the tavern, heading to see his mama.

Dr. Melrose was working with Ellen by having her do different movements so he could evaluate her concussion. "Come on in, Brody. I'm about finished here."

Brody went to Jennifer. "How are you doing?"

"I'm not hurting, but I'm really sore where the stitches are. When can I get out of this bed and join up with my crew?"

"We'll have to get the doctor's opinion, but I think you can get out of bed and begin to walk around the office. The soreness will get better every day, but I don't want you riding a horse for at least a week or more."

Dr. Melrose finished testing Ellen. "Listen up. Ellen can go home. She's doing fine, but I don't want her doing a lot of physical labor. Jennifer, you can get out of bed and walk around the office. If you feel like it tomorrow, you can get dressed and walk outside."

The boy went to his mama and took her by the hand. "Come on, Mama, I'll walk you home."

She was getting up when Jennifer asked, "Are you coming back tomorrow to help me walk outside?"

Ellen started laughing. "I believe that you two just may like each other." Everyone in the room laughed.

Chapter Forty-Eight

WHEN BRODY AND HIS MAMA WERE OUTSIDE and walking down the street, she took hold of his arm. "Son, this ain't the way home."

Brody smiled at his mama. "I know. We have a business to run. Butch and Elmer are no longer at the tavern. The poker dealer said Hermon is at McPherson, so now is the time for us to take control of the business."

"Son, what happened to Butch?"

"He went for his gun, and I shot him. I have a big mess to clean up when we get to the tavern."

"You said that Elmer was also gone. Where did he go?"

"He went to his farm south of town."

The undertaker's wagon was parked in front of the tavern when Brody and his mama arrived. They walked inside in time to see four men lifting the corpse of Butch up.

"Mama, I'll go draw a couple of buckets of water if you'll find a large pan and rags."

Ellen pointed toward the back. "Let's go into the back

room where you can get a fire going in the stove. I'll get the cleaning supplies while you get the water heating on the stove. You made a big mess with Butch, didn't you."

"He had it coming," said Brody, and grabbed two buckets and went outside to the water well.

Brody almost vomited cleaning up the multicolored brain matter on the counter where most of it landed. He next started to mop the floor and cleaning the bottles was last. Ellen inspected the entire area and pointed out a few places that needed more attention.

After the place was clean, Ellen showed Brody how to pour whiskey and beer. He worked the counter and the tables for the rest of the day. The last customer left at eleven that evening, and that's when Brody closed for the day.

He walked his mama home and then went to the hotel for his clothing. Before going back to his home, Brody walked by the tavern to make sure everything was still okay.

Back at home, Ellen was asleep when he went to his room and went to bed.

———

THE FOLLOWING MORNING, Brody ate breakfast with his mama, then cleaned the kitchen while she got ready to head to the tavern. Brody was concerned about Hermon coming back unexpectedly and wanted to be prepared when the man returned.

It was earlier than usual when the mother and son opened the business that morning. While Ellen took inventory of the bar items, Brody went into the back-room to search through Hermon's stuff.

He went after a trash basket and started throwing

Hermon's clothing and such in it. Nothing was found that gave the young man any information about Hermon.

Brody heard talking in the big room and went in to investigate. The dealer that he talked to the day before was in a heated conversation with his mama.

The man stopped talking when Brody came in. "Don't quit talking on my account. By the way, what's your name?"

"I'm Drift Bowden, and I made a deal with Hermon on the gambling. She's now saying that the deal is off."

"Well, she's the owner of the tavern and can make her own agreements," said Brody. "Mama, what's the new agreement on gambling?"

"I'm willing to pay him twenty percent of the house, but no cheating. He seems to have a problem running an honest game."

"Drift, if you don't want to run an honest game, then I suggest you find another place to work. We're changing the way the tavern operates, and my mama is in charge."

"We'll see about that when Hermon gets back and kills the both of you." Brody had enough of this man and came around with a right haymaker that floored the gambler. "Mister, you're walking on thin ice with me. I highly suggest that you get out and don't come back."

The dealer got off the floor and was rubbing his jaw as he walked out of the tavern. "Mama, I suspect that Drift has already sent word to Hermon about what's going on here."

"I know they're close and have worked together before," said Ellen. "Who told you that Hermon went to McPherson?"

"It was Drift. I bet he was lying. I need to go see the telegraph operator and see if he sent Hermon a message."

"He ain't supposed to give you that information, but I know things that will make him tell you what you need," said Ellen.

Brody walked to the telegraph office to find only the operator inside the small building. "Hello, Mr. Wilson. Do you remember who I am?"

"Why, yes I do. You're Thaddeus, Dr. Melrose's assistant. What can I do for you?"

"I understand that you're not supposed to give out information on who or where messages go, but I need to know if anyone has sent any telegrams to Hermon Muller."

"I'm not allowed to give out that information unless it's to the law."

"Well, now, we seem to be at the place where negotiations are in order. My mama has some very private information that she's willing to forget if you give me the information I need."

The man was getting puffed up. "Why, that's blackmail, and I won't stand for it."

Brody put both elbows on the little counter. "Are you sure you want to play this game?"

The operator pointed to the door. "You, sir, can get out of my business."

Brody removed his elbows and stood straight up. "Sure thing, Mr. Wilson. I'm heading back to the tavern so my mama can have a talk with your wife." Brody turned toward the door and pulled it open.

"Hold up! Two telegrams were sent to Hermon in Newton, Kansas. The card dealer sent one message letting Hermon know that Butch was dead. A feller I don't know came in a little while ago and sent him one saying the boy is in town and he killed Butch. Have money ready when he's dead. That's all I know."

"Are you sure they were both sent to Newton?" asked Brody.

"Yep, they were both sent to Newton."

"You said you don't know the second man, but have you seen him around town before?"

"I'm pretty sure he hangs out at the Silver Dollar Saloon. The only thing I can remember that sticks out on the man is the little finger on his left hand is missing."

Brody thought about the man he saw Butch give the slip of paper to. "Thanks, Mr. Wilson, your secret is safe," said Brody, and headed back to talk to his mama.

Chapter Forty-Nine

A COUPLE OF CUSTOMERS WERE HAVING DRINKS at a table when Brody returned to the bar to talk to Ellen. "Mama, Hermon's in Newton. Do you know a man that's missing the little finger on his left hand?"

"Yeah, he's a local thug that does people's dirty work. His name is Thomas McCall, but he goes by Tom. Why do you want to know?"

"He's the man who Hermon hired to kill me for shooting Ludwig. Do you know where I can find Tom?"

"He comes in here occasionally but stays at the Silver Dollar most of the time. You be careful with that one. He's known to have men on his payroll."

"Will you be all right here while I go see if he's at the saloon?"

"Yes, I'll be fine, but I wish you wouldn't go to the Silver Dollar."

"You don't understand. If this man is out to kill me, I have to be the aggressor and take him by surprise. I can't be looking over my back all the time to see who is going to shoot me."

"I'm your mama, and I worry. You go do what you have to do, and I'll be fine here."

Brody wanted to be prepared for the unexpected and walked to the livery stable to get his horse. While the hostler was saddling Brody's pony, the young man asked, "Do you know a feller that stays at the Silver Dollar who is missing the little finger on his left hand?"

"Yep, that would be Tom, but he ain't at the saloon. He rode out this morning heading north. I figured he was going hunting since he took his rifle with him."

Brody thought about what the liveryman said. He wanted to talk to the telegraph operator again before he did anything.

When he walked inside the telegraph office, the operator looked up and reached for a slip of paper. "I have something you need to see."

Brody took the slip of paper and read it. "What do you think this means?"

"I'd say Hermon is telling Tom to wait at a certain place to see if you come looking for him," said the operator.

"That's what I think it's saying. Do you know where the Iron Stob Creek crossing is located?"

"I believe it's about two miles north of here. It's in a shallow valley with open farmland surrounding it. I would be concerned about someone on top of the hill after I crossed the creek if I was you."

Brody was thinking of a plan. "Is there a way I can circle around and come in from the backside of the hill?"

"It's a little farther, but you can turn west at the first crossroads and then north at the Mitchell farm. There's a narrow road that will take you past the creek, and once you cross over the hill, you'll have timber to cover you."

"Thanks for helping me."

He followed the direction and found a lane that he thought the gentleman at the telegraph office had told him about. Another mile and he crossed a creek and that's where Brody removed the safeties off both his guns.

When he was on the hill covered with timber, he left his horse tied to a sapling and started east on foot until he could see a gap in the trees where Tom would be watching.

Brody crept his way through the trees and was almost even with the road when he saw Tom behind a tree with the rifle aimed at the creek crossing.

He was too far away to shoot with a pistol, and the young man needed to get closer. Getting closer could be deadly since Tom had a rifle, and if Brody made any noise, the surprise would be over.

Maybe if he stayed where he was, Tom would get tired of waiting and make a mistake. Brody stayed hidden behind a tree for the longest time, although it was only minutes. This was getting old, and he started looking for a different route to come up to Tom.

Brody retreated the way he had come and circled around so he could come in from the east. Tom wouldn't be expecting anyone from that direction. The new route was northeast of where Tom stood hidden. Staying low and using caution with each step to minimize the noise, the hunter was able to get within thirty feet of Tom.

Brody pulled his pistol and pulled back the hammer. The sound of the metal as it clicked made Tom stiffen up. "Tom, move very slow and turn around."

Tom turned to his left so the man behind him couldn't see him drop his right hand to his pistol. "I ain't done anything to you, mister. If it's money you want, I might have twenty dollars on me."

"I'm the man that killed Ludwig and Butch. You're here to shoot me, so pull iron and try your luck."

"I ain't going to draw on you," said Tom, and turned with the pistol in his hand. Brody began to fire at Tom and in doing so, he felt the sting of a bullet to his left shoulder. Two more shots, and Tom was on the ground bleeding badly.

Brody went to the man and untied the handkerchief from Tom's neck and placed it over one of the holes where the blood was seeping out.

"Tom, was it worth getting killed to work for Hermon?"

"Hermon will kill you when he gets back to Wichita," said Tom with blood running out the side of his mouth.

"When's Hermon coming back to Wichita?"

"Tomorrow." Tom closed his eyes and took his last breath.

Chapter Fifty

WITH THE ADRENALINE FLOWING THROUGH HIS system, Brody didn't realize how bad he was hit until Tom died. The pain became extreme and caused the young man to put his hand to the area that was giving him severe aching. Drawing his blood-covered hand away, the realization that he was shot and needed to get help kicked in with a sense of urgency.

Looking at his shoulder as best as he could revealed that the bullet had went all the way through the muscle without hitting the bone or joint. He ripped the sleeve off his shirt and used it as a bandage to stop the flow of blood.

Brody got in the saddle and headed back to Wichita as fast as he could without causing himself more harm. Even though he wanted to help people, there were times a man had to stand on his own feet and protect himself. That's how he justified shooting men like Tom.

Brody had to slow the horse down to a walk when he felt faint. The one thing that could happen was him falling off his horse. He had to stay awake until he arrived at Dr. Melrose's office.

As he entered town, a man saw the bloodied arm and came out into the street and took hold of the bridle. "Hang in there, mister, and I'll take you to the doctor."

Brody could feel himself sinking in and out of consciousness as the man led the horse to the doctor's office. The stranger tied the horse to the hitch rail and rushed to the door, where he called out for the doctor. The stranger, with the help of Dr. Melrose, helped Brody down off the horse and took him into the office.

Dr. Melrose went to work on the wound and gave Brody medicine to help with the pain. After getting the wound clean and bandaged, the doctor put the injured arm in a sling to keep it out of use.

"Brody, the bullet went through clean, but it's going to be sore and tender for a long time. I suggest that you be very careful and don't try to use your left arm until the hole has time to heal."

Brody sat up. "I have to go see my mama. She's alone at the tavern, and Hermon is coming back from Newton tomorrow. He may try to hurt her if I'm not there for her protection."

Dr. Melrose made a jester with his face. "I'm not sure how effective you'll be with only one arm, but you can try."

Jennifer walked into the room. "Brody, two of my cowhands stayed behind to help me get home when I get released to travel. If you need them, they're available to help."

"Thanks for the offer, Jennifer, but I want your men to help you get home safely."

"Okay, but remember they're here if you need them."

She then walked back out, and he didn't see her anymore.

Brody put his bloody shirt on as best as he could without moving the arm. He walked to his ma's house where he put on a clean shirt with a lot of difficulty and pain. It was now time to go see his mama and let her know what happened and why he got shot.

The town's drinking people must have heard the news that Butch and Hermon were no longer operating the bar. The establishment had doubled in the number of locals that had been coming in, and Ellen was behind the bar filling glasses. A young lady was moving around the room delivering drinks and wiping off tables.

Ellen stopped what she was doing when the injured boy came inside. "Thaddeus, what in the world happened to you?"

"I found the man Hermon paid to kill me, and he shot me in the shoulder before I killed him. Tom told me before he died that Hermon was coming back to Wichita tomorrow. We have to be prepared if he comes to the tavern. I'm down to one arm, but I can still shoot if he comes in here."

Ellen thought for a second. "He may not come here if he knows that Butch is dead. The Mullers have a farm a few miles west of the Arkansas River. He will most likely go there until he can shoot us in the back."

"Do you know of any other men on his payroll that could give us problems?" asked Brody.

"Hermon met with men in the back room, and I never heard any of his conversations. I have a feeling that Ludwig was also working for Hermon, and that's the reason he came here after Ludwig died. He came to protect his investment."

"We have to be ready for whatever he brings with

him," said Brody. "I'm going over to that table in the corner so I can look out the window and also watch both doors."

Ellen started back filling glasses. "If I see him or anyone that I recognize as the men he met with, I'll let you know."

Brody sat down and got his arm as comfortable as he could before he got to thinking about his future. If it wasn't for his mama being here, he would leave today. The time he spent on the run had been so educational to him and his quest of becoming a doctor. He delivered a baby and cared for the mother, and operated on a woman and it saved her life. The town of Kingfisher took him in with open arms, and he saved the life of a newborn baby by finding parents who wanted to adopt it.

He came back here to people harming his mama, men getting paid to kill him, and it's all over a scum of a man named Ludwig Muller.

Brody became bored, and his shoulder began to ache so he would get up and walk around the room. His mama and the new waitress worked the counter and tables like pros.

By dusk, the tavern was booming with men and a few women coming in for drinks. All three of the poker tables were full of men playing different types of card games. He thought about joining in on a game but decided against it.

Back at his corner table, he began to think about Hermon coming back tomorrow. It would probably be close to dark before Hermon arrived. Since he knew that Butch was dead, it wasn't likely he would come here first. With his connection in the criminal element, the likely place would be where he could hire extra help.

He got up and walked to the counter. "Mama, who

would Hermon meet with if he was hiring gunmen to help him do a job?"

She stood thinking for a few moments. A feller standing at the counter drinking a beer chimed in. "I couldn't help but overhear your question. If I was wanting hired guns, I would go see Rosco down at that little bar on the Arkansas River."

"Are you talking about that shack called Lorrie's?" asked Ellen.

"Yeah, Rosco is her man, and he has a long reach around town with the criminal element."

"What about Tom? Who did he work for?" asked Brody.

"Tom's a lowlife that bushwhacks people. The men Rosco has are face-to-face fighters," said the man.

"Thanks for the information. I'm Brody. What's your name?"

"I'm David Thorton, and it's nice to meet the man who killed Butch. He was lower than scum in the bottom of the river."

The two men shook hands, and Brody said to his mama, "I'll be back in a little while. I'm going to have a talk with Rosco."

"You be careful. Lorrie's place has a bad reputation for violence."

Chapter Fifty-One

BRODY DIDN'T WANT TO HURT HIS SHOULDER BY hoisting himself into the saddle, so he walked to Lorrie's dive. He knew where it was located, but had never been there. The route to the place wasn't through the best part of town and that resulted in him taking the safety strap off both guns. He placed his hand on the shoulder holster gun as he passed by people on the street.

The only door on the weather-beaten building was wide open, letting in anything that wanted to enter the place. Its inside looked better than the outside and even had a wood floor covered with sawdust.

Brody stood inside the door, looking around, trying to locate Rosco. Without knowing what the man looked like, he walked to the counter. A black-haired woman came over. "What's on your mind, Gringo?"

"A beer will do if it's cool."

She turned and went down the counter and started getting his beer.

He then thought about the situation he was in. He ordered a beer and would have to hold the mug with his right hand. That could be a problem if he needed to draw a gun.

The woman brought him the beer. "That'll be twenty cents."

Brody put a quarter on the counter. "Tell Rosco that I would like to talk to him."

"What do you want to talk to him about?" she asked.

"Life and death," said Brody with a stern look on his face.

"Wait here." She walked away and spoke to a man at the opposite end of the counter. That man took off, and Brody took a big swallow of the beer. The wait was short when the man came in and motioned for Brody to follow him.

Brody left the mug on the counter, but kept his hand on the gun butt in the shoulder holster. The man he followed took him outside and around to the back of the bar to find two men sitting under an overhang drinking beer.

A short man with a bald head and a beer belly stood up. "I'm Rosco, who are you and what do you want?"

"I'm Brody Connor, and I came here to talk to you about Hermon Muller."

Rosco looked Brody up and down. "Are you the man that killed Ludwig and Butch?"

"Yeah, and I killed the two men Hermon paid to kill me in Indian Territory. He also hired Tom to kill me and that didn't work out for him. Hermon's on his way back to Wichita, and I'm going to confront him face-to-face. I'm here to talk to you about not getting involved."

"Muller hired those two men from Tom. Neither them or Tom are smart enough to hunt down anyone," said Rosco. "Me and the Mullers are not friends but that doesn't matter when it comes to making money."

"I came here today to ask you to turn him down when he comes looking to hire guns to come after me."

"What if I don't turn him down and provide him what he wants?"

Brody was trying not to show fear in his voice. "Then I'll come here for you after I kill your men."

Rosco smiled. "I like you, Brody Connor. A man in my line of business knows a good deal when it comes around. You, young man, are a good deal. I hear that you and your mama are running the bar. If I turn Hermon down, would you be open to me making an offer on the tavern?"

"Rosco, I'm leaving Wichita after I kill my enemies and going to Kansas City for medical school. I'm a healer and want to become a doctor so I can help save lives. You keep your part of the deal, and I'll have my mama sit down with you about buying the bar."

Rosco stood up and stuck out his hand. Brody took it to seal the deal. When they were finished, Rosco said, "Hermon will do anything he can to get even with you over Butch and Ludwig. He's a conniving, evil man who won't confront you to your face."

"What do you think he'll do when he gets to town?"

"He'll do something to even the playing field and try to have you make a mistake. He may be able to hire a gun or two, but I'll help with that. I'm a powerful man with lots of resources. I'll put the word out for no one to hire on with Hermon. The rest will be up to you, Brody Connor."

"Thanks, Rosco. That's more than I could ever ask for."

Rosco held up a finger. "One last thing. Hermon has a house two miles west of town, surrounded by farmland. It's a pain to sneak up on it unless you know how to.

There's an irrigation ditch about a hundred yards behind the barn. A man could crawl down the ditch and get to the house that way. Your only problem is that shoulder."

"Hopefully, I won't have to try that, but I can if I have to. An old Apache I stayed with in the Indian Territory taught me many skills, and I'm hoping I get to Hermon before he knows what's going on."

Rosco cocked his head to one side. "What was the Indian's name?"

"It was William Longtooth."

Rosco started laughing. "I was hoping it was William. You're a lucky man or you did something extraordinary for him to even talk to you. That old man is one of the most fierce fighters I've ever seen."

"William is a good friend and he taught me how to heal with plants, roots, leaves, and other native things. I spent weeks at his house while he taught me the art of fighting and how to call on the Great Spirit for help."

"If William taught you those things, then you are special. Me and you will be great friends, Brody Connor," said Rosco, and stuck out his hand for another shake.

"Thanks for meeting with me, Rosco. I'll tell my mama about your offer."

Rosco started walking. "Let's go inside so I can introduce you to my people." Rosco led the way inside.

"Listen up! Shouted out Rosco. This man is Brody Connor, a great warrior, healer, and my friend. Stay out of his way and leave him alone or you will answer to me."

Brody touched the brim of his hat. "It's nice to meet you all. Thanks again, Rosco."

Brody left the bar with an assurance that Hermon wouldn't be hiring any of Rosco's hired gunhands. He walked to the livery stable and had the hostler saddle his horse. With the help of a chair, he was in the saddle heading west out of town. He wanted to look Hermon's land and house over before the evil man arrived there tomorrow night.

The house was in the slap-dap middle of a hundred acres planted in corn which hadn't been harvested for feed yet. The ditch was dry and he could most likely walk down it with the dried corn stalks giving him cover.

After looking the place over and opening the back door of the barn in case he needed to come through it, Brody rode back to town for supper.

Chapter Fifty-Two

THE TAVERN WAS BUSTLING WITH BUSINESS when Brody came back from Hermon's farm. Ellen was busy at the counter, and the waitress couldn't keep up at the tables. Ellen motioned for her son to come behind the bar.

His mama threw a rag over his shoulder. "Son, work the counter while I help Sharon with the tables."

"I don't know how to work the counter or how much to charge," said Brody. "You need to hire more help."

"Okay, but I need you back here helping me pour drinks. You take care of the beer drinkers, and I'll do the whiskey. Beer is twelve cents and whiskey is twenty cents."

Brody didn't like having to work behind the counter. It took him away from watching for Hermon and that could be deadly for them if he showed up unannounced. Pouring beer in the mugs with only one hand had its disadvantages, and there was so much foam that he had to let the mug sit until he could top them off.

Ellen came over to him. "Let me show you what to

do." She tilted the mug and poured the beer slow so it slid down the inside edge of the glass.

"Mama, I only have one hand. I can't do it like you can."

"You can pour whiskey with one hand, and I'll do the beer."

Brody began to pour the whiskey along the counter and fill glasses for the girl waiting on tables. It was after midnight before the last customers left, and they could close the business for the night.

His mama was counting the cash drawer as Brody pulled chairs out of the way so Sharon could sweep.

Ellen put the money in her pocket. "Let's stop for the night and go home. We can finish up in the morning."

Brody stayed alert as he walked home with his mama. His shoulder hurt, but he pushed past the pain and kept going. When they were home, he said, "I'm going to Dr. Melrose's office in the morning so he can clean and redress my wound. Then I'll come back here and escort you to the tavern."

"Son, I don't think anything will happen in the morning, now go to your room and get some rest."

Brody couldn't get comfortable and go to sleep because of the continuing ache in the shoulder. He got out of bed, took the medicine pouches that William had given him to the kitchen, where he ground up some of the ingredients with a touch of water to make a paste.

He loosened the bandage enough to apply the paste, then went back to bed. The medicine began to work and he went to sleep. Although the shoulder pain eased up, it didn't go away. He kept waking up and moving around so he could sleep.

Brody felt bad when he woke up from the lack of rest because of his aching shoulder. Getting dressed was an issue, and he finally gritted his teeth and went through getting his clothes on. Dr. Melrose should be in his office by now and that was where he was headed.

Walking seemed to take his mind off the shoulder and gave him time to plan out his day. Hermon coming into town later this afternoon consumed his thoughts until he entered the doctor's office.

Jennifer was sitting at the window in the reception room when he entered.

"Good morning, Brody."

"Hi Jennifer. You're looking wonderful."

"Thanks, Brody. You look like that shoulder is bothering you today."

Brody tried to smile. "It aches and I need a little relief."

"Dr. Melrose is in the backroom. Maybe he can give you something to ease the pain."

"I'll be back," said Brody, and headed to the backroom.

Dr. Melrose met Brody when he entered the examining room.

"Good morning, Brody. Is that shoulder about to drive you crazy?"

"It's really bothering me. I had to put a poultice on it last night so I could get a little sleep."

"Have a seat, and I'll remove the bandage and have a look."

Dr. Melrose cleaned the wound and applied more iodine before he applied clean bandages. He went to the medicine cabinet and came back with a small bottle. "Here's some laudanum to drink when it starts hurting you. I suggest that you move it some to help with the soreness."

"I don't think I should use the medicine, I'm expecting trouble later today, and I need to be my best."

"You keep it to use when you need to get some sleep. The wound is looking fine, and whatever it was you made the poultice out of, worked to eliminate any infection," said Dr. Melrose.

"That was something I learned while living with an Indian healer while I was away," said Brody. "Thanks, Doctor. I best be going to escort my mama to work."

"Come by tomorrow and I'll clean and put clean dressings on the holes. You be careful later today when Hermon comes to town. Although I don't think he'll make a play against you to your face. The man's a bully, and he will either get someone to do his dirty work or he will try to sneak up on you."

"I'll be ready for whatever he brings to me."

Dr. Melrose touched the sling. "Son, you may want to remove that sling later today. If he sees your arm in a sling, he may try to use it against you."

"I think that's good advice. I'll see you later, Doctor."

Brody walked home and found the house empty. He wasn't concerned since his mama said last night that she could walk to work by herself. But he took off to make sure she got there safe. Before leaving, he removed the sling and moved his arm to loosen it up.

The door to the tavern was locked, and no one came to the door when he pounded on it. Brody walked around to the rear of the building to find the back door open and the doorjamb destroyed.

An uneasy feeling came over the young man as he pulled his gun and started into the back room of the tavern. Right before he entered the large room, a strange feeling came over him so much that sweat formed on his forehead. What was waiting on him on the other side of the door?

Brody saw a coat hanging on a peg. He took it down and placed it on his hurt arm where he could pitch it into the room. With the door ajar, he placed his foot where he could open the door and pitched the coat. Pain shot through his shoulder, but that didn't stop him.

Guns were firing from two different locations, and Brody was shooting at the muzzle fire from the guns. One man was down and the other one was still firing when Brody's bullet hit dead center in the man's chest, and the shooting stopped. Brody holstered the gun and drew his second pistol before he went into the room to investigate.

What he found almost made him sick to his stomach. He had seen both of the men yesterday when he went to talk to Rosco. The man had double-crossed him and took Hermon's money. He warned Rosco what would happen and now the local crime boss was on his bad side.

The bigger problem was the absence of his mama. Had she been here and someone taken her away? "Was she someplace in town shopping or at the bank making a deposit?"

Brody walked to the damaged back door, and while looking around, he saw wagon tracks behind the building. The ground where the back of the wagon was parked had footprints and one set was a small print and one a large print.

His mama was loaded into the back of a wagon and carried away down the alley. Brody walked the route the wagon had taken. It turned south, and he continued to follow, then he stopped and reloaded the pistol he used inside the tavern.

Chapter Fifty-Three

THE WAGON HAD TURNED WEST, AND IT LOOKED like the driver was making the horses go faster by the way they were tearing up the soil with their hooves. Suddenly, the tracks blended in with more tracks. This road was the stage route and all the horses using it had the road torn up so badly that he couldn't tell which tracks were from the wagon.

Brody walked to the livery stable where he asked the hostler to saddle his horse. He would ride to the farm that he looked at yesterday, but that location was also given to him by Rosco who was most likely setting him up to be shot.

Brody rode on and wanted to see if the wagon had turned into the lane that went to the house. He didn't feel comfortable being in the open like he was since someone with a rifle could shoot him.

A wagon had turned down the lane, and Brody thought back to what the double crosser had told him. Rosco made it a focal point to tell the young man about the ditch where he could crawl to the house. This was a planned setup, and he wasn't going to fall for it.

Leaving his horse at the road, Brody started to the house by walking down one of the rows of corn. By bending over, and getting as low as possible, he made his way within thirty yards of the house. The front of the house looked like it did yesterday, but he wanted to see more and circled around to the side and that's when he saw the wagon inside the barn.

A gambling man liked a sure bet, and today he made the bet that men were waiting to shoot him as he crawled to the house by way of the ditch. Moving back to the front of the house, Brody ran to the front door and went inside. After searching each room, and not finding his mama, Brody had to think about what to do.

Maybe he could take the men by surprise and find out where they took his mama. He went out the front door and went back into the cornfield so he could get beside the barn.

He ran to the open barn doors and slid under the wagon bed. Pain shot through his shoulder, and he had to stay put as he exercised the arm. The back door was still open from yesterday, and he made his way to it.

Hunkered down behind ricks of wood were two men waiting to kill him as he came out of the irrigation ditch. Brody eased out of the door and got into position before he pulled his gun.

"Howdy, men."

Both men stood up and reached to draw their guns. Brody shot one man and had the other one covered before he had his gun out. "Ease that hog leg out slow like molasses in the winter," said Brody.

The man had his hand close to his gun. "I ain't going to try anything."

Brody cocked back the hammer. The man's eyes got bigger, and he swallowed. "Drop it on the ground or you get the same as your partner."

The man eased the gun out of the holster, dropped it to the ground and raised both his arms. "Mister, we were just doing what we were hired to do. It wasn't personal."

Brody kept the gun on the man. "It's personal to me. You answer my questions, and I may let you live. Now, what did you do with the woman from the tavern?"

"A man met us by the river and took her with him."

"Who do you work for?"

The man was getting fidgety. "Mister, I'm a dead man if I tell you anymore."

"You have a chance to ride away if you tell me what I want to know. If you don't, I'm going to kill you."

"I work for Rosco and that other man has the woman at Lorrie's bar."

"Leave your gun on the ground and take off. If I ever see you again, I'll shoot you like I would a rabid skunk." The man took off, and Brody walked back to his horse. As he was leaving the farm he saw the man in the wagon going south.

Brody wanted to kick himself, Rosco already had the plan in action when he met with the man yesterday. Brody didn't like being lied to or double-crossed. He had actually shook to seal the deal and that would be what was going to get Rosco killed. But first he had to find out where they had his mama. He doubted Hermon would have her at Lorrie's bar. They had to have someplace else with less traffic.

The ride back seemed to take forever as the anticipation grew stronger as he approached town. Brody found a place where he could sit on his horse and watch the bar. A few men entered and then he saw a large man that didn't fit in with the men he saw yesterday. This man could be Hermon and he could take Brody where his mama was being kept. The man kept looking from side to side as he made his way to a house on a hill.

Staying hidden for now was the smart thing to do as he kept track of the man and saw him go inside a house. The young fighter was getting ready to move when he saw the man leave the house and walked to the house next door. He only stayed in there a few minutes until he came out and started into town.

Which house was his mama in and how many men were in there with her? As far as he knew, she was safe but the man walking into town wasn't. Brody took off and headed down a parallel street until he thought he was ahead of Hermon.

By dismounting and leaving his horse in an alley, he could wait until Hermon came closer and surprise the big man.

"Hello, Hermon," said Brody, and stepped out from between two buildings.

Hermon stopped and put his hand inside his jacket. "Who are you and what do you want?"

"I'm the man who killed your sorry, overbearing brother. You stole the tavern from my mama and let your bully hit her. Now it's your time to try me on. I see that you already have the gun in your hand, so pull it if you ain't too yellow."

Hermon flinched, and the gun started out, but he was too slow. Brody had his gun out, and the first shot hit the man in the chest with enough force to make him take a step backward. The second shot caused Hermon's fingers to release the gun, and it fell to the ground, and he followed, holding his chest.

Brody reloaded his gun before he went through Hermon's pockets and discovered a roll of money. He mounted up and rode toward the two houses where he figured his mama was being kept.

Chapter Fifty-Four

Both houses looked abandoned when Brody eased his way along the riverbank behind the residences. The shoulder was hurting but not enough that he wanted to stop. Running up the riverbank to the back door of the first house, Brody leaned on the back wall trying to hear of any movement inside the structure.

He made his way along the building until he could see inside a window. The room was empty and so was the next room. Brody walked back to the back door, and it opened without any resistance. After searching the entire house, he watched the second one to see if there was any movement. Again, there was nothing, and he left the first house and entered the one that Hermon had come out of. There was a bag in the bedroom with a change of clothing, three hundred dollars, and the deed to the tavern.

Brody opened the deed and there was his mother's name on it as the owner. Ludwig or Hermon's name was not on it.

The rest of the house didn't turn up any evidence that

his mama had been there. Where was his mama being held?

He had to check out Lorrie's place, but that was going to be difficult. The odds were against him, especially with the hurt shoulder. Then he thought about Jenniffer and her cowboys. Maybe if he had them as his backup it would make a big difference. Brody walked back to his horse and had only ridden two blocks when two men stepped out in front of him. "Rosco sent us to tell you he's willing to make a trade."

"What kind of trade?"

"He said to bring the deed to the old farmhouse and he will trade your mama for the deed," replied the man.

"Let's do it," said Brody, and moved his horse forward.

"Not so fast. Rosco wants us to make sure you have the deed."

Brody did something that sent pain through his shoulder. He used that arm to remove the deed from his shirt pocket so he could keep his right hand close to his gun.

"Here's the deed. Now, let's get this started."

The man reached out his hand. "Hand it over so we can see it."

Brody put it back in his pocket. "This is all you get. Either we make the trade or we go to war."

"Be at the farmhouse in one hour or the deal's off," said the man, and they turned and walked away.

Brody took off to see Jennifer. He was coming up with a plan on the way there. He pulled up in front of the doctor's office to see three horses tied to the porch post. Inside was two cowboys waiting on Jennifer to come out.

Brody walked through the examining room and found her pulling on her boots.

"Jennifer, I could use some help. Some bad men have my mama at a farmhouse and want to trade her for the deed to the tavern."

Jennifer pulled the boot on and stood up. "I told you we would help. What do you want us to do?"

"The house is surrounded by dried cornstalks and the wind is out of the northwest. We put your men in the cornfield where they can set fire to the corn. I'll ride in on a wagon and make the trade. As soon as we leave in the wagon, your men set fire to the cornfield. That will smoke the men out of the house, and I'm going to teach them a lesson."

Jennifer took his hand into hers. "Let's go tell my men the plan so they can get in position. I'll ride in the back of the wagon and keep you covered with a rifle."

"I would rather you be in the cornfield with your rifle so you can cover the front door of the house. You won't be in pistol range and can leave out if things go wrong."

Jennifer got in front of Brody and leaned in with her eyes on his. She kissed him once on the lips, turned, and left with her men. Brody stood where he was, taking in the moment, smiled, and went to the livery stable to rent a buggy or wagon. He had to hurry to be at the house in the allotted timeline that the men told him to arrive.

Brody turned down the lane to the house and saw Jennifer standing in the corn field with a rifle pointed at the house. As he entered the front yard, he went ahead and turned the buckboard around so it would be heading out.

Keeping the buckboard between the house and himself, Brody called out, "I have the deed right here." He waved it in the air. "Send out my mama, and we can make the exchange."

The door opened, and two men came out carrying rifles. "Amigo, bring the paper here."

Brody stood his ground. "That's not going to happen. Let me see my mama."

Rosco came out on the porch with Ellen in front of him. "I have decided that I don't want to pay for the tavern. Bring me the deed for your mama to sign, and the two of you will be free to go."

"Rosco, you're not a man to be trusted. You bring her to me, and I'll meet you halfway with the deed. We make the exchange and leave."

"No, no, no. Jimmy will bring her to you, and you will give him the deed," said Rosco. "I don't trust you, Brody Connor the healer."

"Fine, send her on out. I have the paper and ink in the buggy."

He knew that as soon as his mama signed the deed, Rosco and the other man would start shooting. Bending over and picking up a rock the size of a fist to hold the paper down, he unfolded the deed and laid it where his mama could sign it.

Brody took one step to the side so he would have a clear shot at the men escorting his mama. The man pushed the little woman along, and when they were near, Brody said, "Mama, sign the deed." She picked up the fountain pen and dipped it in the inkwell. Brody pulled his gun and shot the man standing behind his mama in the head. He turned the gun toward the porch and was firing at Rosco when he saw the other man go down. Jennifer could be heard off to the side firing her rifle.

Rosco ran back inside the house, and Brody picked up his mama and put her in the wagon seat. He could still hear Jennifer's rifle fire shot after shot into the house, and he slapped the horse on the butt, causing it to take off.

Chapter Fifty-Five

BRODY RAN INTO THE CORNFIELD ABOUT THE time guns started firing from inside the house. He lay on the ground and reloaded the spent shells in the gun. The shooting quieted down for a few moments and then he heard shooting from the rear of the dwelling.

Smoke was beginning to drift toward the residence when there was more guns being fired in the rear of the house. In another minute, the fire had reached the barn and flames were shooting into the air higher than the roof on the house.

Brody stood up, waiting on the men in the domicile to make their move. Finally, the door flew open, and out ran two men. Jennifer dropped the first man, and Brody shot the second one.

"Rosco, come on out, and I'll give you a chance to live."

"You come and get me," yelled Rosco.

"I'm giving you a chance to face me, or you can burn to death in that house. The choice is yours."

The fire caught the back of the house, and Brody

could see Jennifer's two cowboys taking aim on the structure. "I'm coming out," hollered Rosco. He came out with his hands up and rushed off the porch to get away from the heat.

"I give up. You can take me to the law."

"That don't work for me," said Brody. "The only way out is to kill me."

Jennifer fired her gun, and a man tumbled out of the front window. Rosco went for his gun, but Brody was waiting on him to try something. Rosco had cleared leather when the first bullet hit him in the chest. He took a step backward and raised the gun, but the second shot tore through his neck with such force that he fell over backward onto his back, with blood squirting like a fountain.

Brody walked up to Rosco, and he was already dead.

"There's three more dead in the backyard," said one of the cowboys. "I suggest we leave here before the fire starts cooking their flesh. I never have liked to smell humans burn."

Brody and the two men walked down the lane and met up with Jennifer. When they made it to the road, there sat Ellen in the buckboard.

"Mama, I think the tavern has caused us enough problems. I recommend you sell it to the highest bidder and move to Kansas City with me," said Brody.

"I'll sell the tavern, but this is my home and I don't want to move. I would only get in your way of becoming a doctor. Your future is worth more to me than life itself," said Ellen. "As for selling the tavern, I've already had a good offer by a well-known businessman."

Brody went to Jennifer and held out his hands. She came into his outstretched arms and put her arms around his neck and kissed him. "That was for saving my life, Dr. Brody Connor."

He smiled and returned the kiss. "That was for saving my life."

She turned to her two hired hands. "Boys, mount up and let's head for home. We've had enough fun for the day."

Brody climbed into the seat with his mama and started back to town.

"Son, what're you going to do with those dead men back there?"

"I'll stop by the county sheriff's office and let him know the men are back there," said Brody.

"Drop me off at home so I can clean up while you go see the sheriff and take the wagon back. Then I want you to come to the bank with me to talk about Mr. Thompson purchasing the tavern. He's the bank's president and is wanting the building for a new business."

"That's great." The boy reached over and patted his mama on the back.

He did the things he told his mama he was going to do and went with her where she made a deal to sale the tavern.

Brody stayed in Wichita for five more days until he was satisfied that his mama would be safe and well.

Each of the five days were spent with him helping at the doctor's office and studying Dr. Melrose's medical books. On the morning Brody was leaving for Kansas City, Dr. Melrose came to the train station.

"Brody, I have for you a gift that I want you to take with you," said Dr. Melrose. "Every time you use it, I want you to remember where you came from and where you're going. You're going to make a fine doctor, and I'm very proud of you."

"Thanks, Doctor. You've been my inspiration and motivation through the journey and I appreciate you taking me in and giving me the opportunity to learn," said Brody.

"Here comes your train," said Dr. Melrose. "You can open your gift on the train. Safe travels and stay in touch."

Dr. Melrose walked off, and Brody stood watching his friend and mentor go. The engine came by puffing steam as it slowed to a stop. The future doctor stepped on the passenger car and went inside to find a seat.

He couldn't wait to see what the good doctor had given him. Inside the box was a black doctor bag and on the outside was a little plaque, *Dr. Brody Connor*.

Chapter Fifty-Six

BRODY SPENT TWO YEARS IN MEDICAL SCHOOL and graduated at the top of his class from the Kansas City School of Medicine. On commencement day, he took to the stage to give a speech to his graduating class, and there sat his mama and Dr. Melrose in the front row.

Brody had no idea they were coming on his special day, and he was getting to share it with the two people who made this possible.

After the ceremony was over and Brody was spending time with his mama and Dr. Melrose. The president of the school came up to them with two men.

"Excuse me, Dr. Connor," said the president. "These two fine gentlemen are the two leading doctors from Saint Louis, and they want to speak with you."

"Dr. Melrose and Mama, would you excuse me for a few moments? This won't take long."

Brody walked off with the two men, who offered him a job in their hospital in Saint Louis. He politely turned them down and came back to his special guests.

"Son, did those men offer you a job?" asked Ellen.

"Yes, they did, but I'm not interested. I want to go west and help poor people who are trying to settle in this beautiful country."

Dr. Melrose shook his head and started laughing. "This young doctor is going to burn a path across the plains wider than a herd of buffalo."

The following morning, Brody, Ellen, and Dr. Melrose boarded the train to Wichita.

Brody had worked for a hospital in Kansas City in between his classes and homework. By saving his money, he was able to buy a riding horse and a pack horse, all the provisions he would need, including medication and tools of the trade.

Four days after arriving in Wichita, young Dr. Brody Connor adjusted the shoulder holster under his left arm and buckled on the holster on his right hip. He tied a handkerchief around his neck and put the black hat on top of his head before he walked into the kitchen and kissed his mama goodbye.

"Son, let me know where you hang out your shingle. I may want to come see you."

"Mama, I love you," said Brody, and kissed her cheek. He walked out carrying his doctor bag and mounted up, heading south toward Indian Territory.

He had never said anything to his mama about Betsy, who was his girlfriend when he lived in Kingfisher. She had written him five months ago, telling him that she fell in love with a man and was going to marry him.

Brody was glad she was happy and he wasn't heading to Kingfisher, but rather on south to Central Texas to see Jennifer. She had been on his mind for the past two years, and they had exchanged letters every month since he was away at school. The Great Spirit had a way of putting people together.

A Look at Book Two

A Search For Justice

He became a doctor to heal, but when justice calls, Brody Connor answers.

Fresh out of the Kansas City School of Medicine and top of his class, Brody Connor turns down a promising career to find *her*. Jennifer—the woman who once helped him save his mother and stole his heart—has gone silent. Her letters stopped months ago. Now, the only thing Brody knows for certain is that he needs answers.

His search leads him through Fort Worth and into the rugged heart of Central Texas, where he learns a devastating truth: raiders have struck the ranch Jennifer called home. Her father and ranch hands are dead. She's been kidnapped. Armed with a healer's hands and a warrior's training, Brody must rely on the skills taught to him by an old Indian fighter to uncover who took Jennifer. With every clue he uncovers, the stakes rise.

Can a young doctor trained to save lives become the man who takes them to bring justice? Or will his search for the woman he loves end in *blood and betrayal?*

AVAILABLE JANUARY 2026

About the Author

Monty was born and raised in Southeastern Oklahoma in the small town of Sawyer, which is nested along the banks of the Kiamichi River. He's owned horses and cattle, riding the former and working the latter. Over the years, he formed a deep connection and respect for the Old West and the courageous folks who braved the wild frontier.

Monty is an avid reader and is particularly enthusiastic when it comes to Western authors and novels. His love of reading sparked his desire to write his first short story. He loves writing about real places and landmarks from the 1800s. In college, he wrote a ten-page paper about his grandmother, born in 1886, who married at fourteen and took in five orphaned nieces and nephews shortly thereafter. Monty's love for history and penchant for storytelling earned him an A+, and he hasn't looked back since.

Now retired, he loves to travel, fish, spend time with his four grandkids, and tell stories. He looks for inspiration for future books wherever he goes, and he is a member of the Western Writers of America Inc.

www.montygarnerauthor.com